THE VILLAINESS IS THE HEROINE'S BIGGEST FAN

악녀는 여주의 1호팬!

WRITTEN BY CHENOBE

EDITIO

PUBLISHING

The Villainess is the Heroine's Biggest Fan

© Chenobe

Cover Illustration by 900

악녀는 여주의 1호팬! by 체노베

Copyright © 2021 by 체노베

All rights reserved.

This English edition was published by Editio Publishing LLC in 2025 by arrangement with DAYS ENTER CORPORATION c/o KCC (Korea Copyright Center Inc.), Seoul, Korea.

ISBN 978-1-959742-61-6 (Print)

Printed in the United States of America

https://editiopublishing.com/

THE VILLAINESS IS THE HEROINE'S BIGGEST FAN

CONTENTS

CHAPTER
ONE HUNDRED
AND SIX

Ever since that day, Aria had started to tease me. She mentioned Ethen at every chance she got, poking fun at me.

"Oh wait, is that necklace from Lord Ethen too?"

"H-how am I supposed to know that?"

I nearly spat out my tea, but all my irritation elicited from her was a comment that I was cute.

"Ah, yes, it's from Lord Ethen. He gave it to Lady Mary on her birthday last year."

I fidgeted with it, wondering if I should take it off. "He probably didn't mean anything by it anyway."

If it was my last birthday, he'd probably chosen some random gift because he couldn't ignore his fiancée's birthday but couldn't be bothered to pick one out himself.

"That looks too impressive to be a random gift."

"Just because it's expensive doesn't mean that it was a sincere gift. I don't even like necklaces that much, anyway," I said, feeling the necklace. "I prefer something more practical or meaningful. I've got plenty of money and gems already." Having purposefully downplayed his gift, I changed the subject smoothly. "I can buy whatever I want. That's why I help other people, invest my money... and things like that. That's what gives me joy."

"Even if you say that, I can't let you have your way this time."

Tsk. I pouted. "What are you doing, exactly, that you're so bent on hiding it? Don't you trust me?"

"Of course I trust you," Aria said, waving her hands about. "Frankly, I could tell you right now... but that would ruin the fun."

"I don't like surprises," I muttered unhappily. It was so frustrating to know that she was up to something but not know what it was. "You could just tell me."

"You'll find out soon enough."

But how am I supposed to know how long it will be? It could be days, weeks, or even months. I glared at Aria with an offended look.

"I won't change my mind because you look at me like that," Aria said, laughing my behavior off.

"And what was with the sheet..." I hesitated as I was about to mention the sheet music, afraid she would think I had searched her room.

"I'm sorry?"

"I-it's nothing. I'm just curious about where you've been going."

Aria thought for a moment. "Uh... let's say I've been meeting someone new," she said, her words charged with meaning. She looked over at me. "I've been wondering about something."

"What is it?"

"Lady Iris told me that you've liked Lord Ethen from a young age."

Cough, cough!

It was a good thing I wasn't drinking my tea at that moment. If I had, I'd likely have spewed it in Aria's face.

I was the one who was supposed to be the bystander in Aria's romance. *Why does it feel like things are going the other way around?*

"That was when I was little. All little girls love handsome boys, don't they?" I said, doing my best to pull myself together.

In the novel, Ethen had been such a pitiful character. He'd been harassed from an early age by his atrocious fiancée, and his father expected great things from him but never praised him for anything he did. He broke up with his fiancée and escaped from his father's expectations, and his life seemed to be looking up. And then he ended up getting rejected. He really had been a miserable person.

Mary had been haughty even after she'd grown up a little. No doubt she'd been no better as a child.

Imagining what she must have been like at that age, I said, "He was no Prince Charming, but he was the most talented of my acquaintances and handsome as well. Of course I liked him."

Mary had liked Ethen, of course, but not with the exciting passion one would feel toward a first love. Perhaps she had only wanted him so she could show him off or feel gratification from having him.

"I obviously couldn't let anyone else have him."

She had assumed that Ethen was hers no matter what and that he was the only one suited to be her fiancé. Her feelings were no doubt closer to the sort of greed one would feel for jewelry or an achievement than real love.

"Hahaha. I suppose children tend to think that way. Still, I think it's amazing."

"What do you mean?"

"Being engaged and still liking someone you've known for so long. All of it."

I clenched my fists on my knees under the table. I couldn't lie to her forever, but I couldn't figure out when would be the right time to tell her. If I didn't, these uncomfortable conversations would only continue. *What do I do?*

"There's nothing amazing about it. I've grown out of it. To be honest, I'm growing tired of him."

I wish Aria were not so quick-witted. She had recognized my feelings as well as Ethen's much too easily and was behaving as though she wanted us to be together. That was to be expected—she could clearly see that we liked each other. Wishing for us to break up would have been weirder.

But the relationship among Ethen, Aria, and me wasn't that simple. I knew too much to do everything the way I wanted.

"Loving someone you've known all your life is something you only see in fairy tales. You never know when your feelings will change." I pretended not to be interested in Ethen. Even if it would be of no use, this felt like the least I could do. I hoped she would think that I was complaining much like I usually did, capricious as I was. I studied Aria's reaction carefully.

"Ethen, my son," the duchess said, looking excited.

"Yes, Mother."

"So, I'll finally be able to see Lady Mary again two days from now. It's been so long. She used to love these cookies as a child. I wonder if she still does." The duchess had avoided seeing Mary for years, hating the very sight of her, but now she looked excited by the prospect.

"Does the benefit of a marriage with the house of the marquess matter to you more than your son's future?"

When she had met Mary last, the duchess had seen her behave in the rudest way imaginable. She'd gotten angry at the duke, and that was a memory Ethen would take with him to the grave.

"You'll be Duke Frangert to the end of your days, not the father of my son."

Ethen had known that his parents were not on the best of terms, but the duchess was a kind soul. She'd never once complained about anything to her husband, so seeing her so angry had come as quite a shock to Ethen.

After that day, the duchess had refused to see Mary at all. Before the incident, she had sent letters and gifts from time to time, because Mary was Ethen's fiancée and excuses could be made on account of her young age. But afterward, she stopped communicating with Mary altogether except on the usual occasions like birthdays.

"You should never be too quick to judge a person. Don't you agree?" After hearing news about Mary at a salon, however, she'd decided to trust her again. "I was frankly a little... worried about her when she debuted, but I guess I shouldn't have been."

She'd heard that Mary had aided her father in his business ventures, and in recent months she'd refrained from attending the social gatherings she loved so much, choosing to stay quiet. Things also seemed to be going very well between her and Ethen, which meant that the duchess probably didn't need to avoid her anymore.

"Ethen?"

"Oh, right. Mother." Ethen, who had an uncertain look on his face, did his best to smile.

"Don't you agree?"

"Yes. I've been learning a lot from her recently. She does her best in everything she undertakes, and that always makes me want to help."

Ethen took a bite from the cookie the duchess held out. Mary had loved these cookies when she was around ten.

"I like these. But I like you too, so I'll make a special exception and give you one."

Ethen recalled the young Mary holding out the cookie as if she was giving him some fabulous gift.

"Thank you, but I don't really like cookies."

"It's good."

Frankly, he hadn't really liked Mary back then. He had felt duty bound to be nice to her since his father had picked her out for him, but that was about it. In fact, he'd been a bit scared of the girl, who obviously liked him and didn't bother to hide it.

"Why aren't you eating it? I'm offering it to you. Do you not like me?"

"It's not like that."

Not wanting the cookie she'd taken a bite out of, he lied to her, saying he didn't like cookies, which made her cry.

"Waaah!"

Ethen smiled faintly as he recalled this incident.

"I haven't held a party in a while, and I'm a little rusty. I'm sorry for calling you over. You must be busy."

"Don't mention it. Of course I should be helping. I had nothing important at hand."

After the fight with the duke, the duchess had refused to even talk with her husband. But she'd accepted his request for her son's sake.

From what the servants told her, it was clear that Ethen had fallen for Mary. That meant that the duchess had no reason to oppose this engagement or a marriage between them. She would do everything she could to help him as his mother. That was the reason she was holding this party—she wanted to show Ethen and Mary off to people and let them know that Lady Mary would soon become a part of the duke's family.

"Even if we hold the engagement ceremony next year, we need to show people that Lady Mary is special to us." She knew about the rumors secretly going around about the two of them. She was planning on making the party grander to prove those rumors false. "I'm worried she might feel uncomfortable around me."

"She has no reason to feel that way about you. Please don't be concerned."

The duchess smiled at Ethen. "It's a relief to hear you say that." She hadn't met Mary for years and had avoided her openly during that time. That made her a touch concerned, but Ethen's reassurances allowed her to relax a little.

Ethen, on the other hand, was as anxious as could be.

CHAPTER ONE HUNDRED AND SEVEN

He felt certain that Mary would not be as rude in the duchess' presence as she had been years ago. She still spoke in a testy way, but she no longer acted rude. However, there was something else that Ethen was worried about.

After he had gotten her to agree to a month's reprieve, he wrote to her daily. Trying not to make her uncomfortable, he avoided mentioning the agreed-upon month and simply filled the letters with everyday topics.

He hadn't gotten a single reply. He wasn't sure if she had even read the letters.

Ethen was anxious that she would be awkward toward him rather than the duchess, but he hid his concern and forced himself to smile.

"She was never rude to you specifically, Mother."

"Well, yes, I suppose..."

The duchess recalled the last time she'd seen Mary, and she frowned slightly. It had been the year after Mary's debut. At the time, the duchess often invited her to the mansion.

This was partly to show off the relationship she had with the House of Bell, and back then, she hadn't viewed Mary negatively. Mary was soon to marry the duchess' son, and though she could be unruly at times, the duchess could be forgiving on account of her youth.

The trouble Mary caused that day, however, was inexcusable despite her age.

The duchess' party had been going on peacefully for a few hours when disaster struck.

"Ahhhhh!"

Someone screamed loudly, attracting everyone's attention. Everyone fell silent at the sight that greeted them, staring at the person who had screamed.

"How dare you ignore me?"

"Ahhh! Somebody help!"

Mary held another lady by the hair, shaking her violently. The reason was simple: the girl had spoken ill of her behind her back.

Backbiting was extremely common in high society, where people smiled at each other but turned vicious as soon as their backs were turned, so most nobles could not understand why Mary was reacting this way. Everyone gossiped about everyone else. This was something to be ignored rather than dragged out into the light so crudely.

"*Mary, are you out of your mind?*" May said, his face paling as he rushed over and pulled Mary away. However, a handful of the lady's hair had already been pulled out.

The guests at the party had all been staring, not daring to do anything to stop her.

Sob...! The lady began to wail in plain sight, obviously feeling humiliated.

Chaos ensued at the mansion, of course. Even the duchess, who had dominated high society for years and had a wealth of experience, was at a loss. Only May had the presence of mind to try to stop Mary. He gripped Mary by the arm, doing whatever he could to calm the situation.

"*You apologize right now! What are you thinking?*"

"*I didn't do anything wrong!*"

Instead of apologizing, Mary tried to grab at the girl's hair again. May stopped her, of course, but that didn't improve the situation. The lady engaged to the heir of the duke had just done something terrible at a party hosted by the duchess.

This was mortifying for both houses.

"*P-please apologize. Since this happened at such a public event, I will not hold it against you if you will do so.*"

The count's daughter, who had recovered her composure after a bout of crying, extended a friendly hand first. This was only for her own reputation, of course, and not because she was really willing to forgive Mary. She wanted to make up for bursting into tears in public and avoid making an enemy of the marquess' house. Unfortunately, Mary wasn't smart enough to realize this.

"You should be the one apologizing. Did you think you wouldn't have to pay the price after talking about me behind my back?" Mary fumed as she tossed the hair she'd pulled out at the count's daughter. That was a scene the guests at the party would remember for years to come.

"I sincerely apologize. I apologize for her behavior."

It was May who had to handle the situation. Dragging his furious twin away, he bid an early goodbye to the duchess.

"I apologize, Duchess Frangert. I think I'll have to take her home early."

"Y-yes. You do that," the duchess said with an effort, still unable to process her shock.

The party's jovial mood seemed restored after Mary left, but the duchess knew that this was far from the truth.

"My goodness, I heard she was reckless, but this...!"

"The duchess must be so humiliated."

"It was so barbaric of her! She grabbed a lady by the hair!"

Though the party looked peaceful on the outside, the conversations were anything but friendly. They were talking about Mary, of course, and many were even badmouthing the duchess while pretending to be worried about her. The duchess had held the party to make a good impression on her guests, but she'd ended up with a marred reputation instead.

After that day, the duchess stopped contacting Mary altogether. She'd shouted at her husband, demanding to know how such an atrocious lady could be their son's fiancée.

However, nothing changed. The duke treated her like a fool, asking her what better match there could be than the daughter of the House of Bell. And as for Mary, despite humiliating the duchess in front of the guests, she didn't send a single letter of apology.

"Well, I suppose," the duchess said.

Just because it hadn't been the duchess' hair that Mary had grabbed didn't mean that all could be forgiven. Still, the duchess wasn't as angry as she had been. And it wasn't because she believed that Mary would have seen the error of her ways completely.

"Are you being protective of her because she's your fiancée? Haha!"

The duchess had not opposed the engagement because she'd felt humiliated. What mattered to her most was her son's happiness. It mattered more than the fact that Mary didn't seem to be making much trouble lately or that rumors said she had caught the emperor's attention.

"I'm not. I'm just... describing her as she is."

"I'm looking forward to seeing her," the duchess said, covering her mouth and laughing when she saw the confusion on her son's face.

Her heart had ached for her son as he continued the engagement he didn't even want because he wanted to be acknowledged by the duke. But over the past few months, her son had been behaving like a young man falling in love for the very first time.

She had nearly dropped her teacup in astonishment when she heard that Ethen, who had been so afraid of his father and so fearful of angering him, had lent Mary the duke's voice recorder without permission. Ethen had never done his best in the hunting competition—because he disliked drawing attention, but this year he had gone out on a limb to win. That was also very surprising.

The duchess decided that there must be a reason why Ethen had suddenly fallen in love with Mary, and she made up her mind to support their relationship, forgetting the things that had happened in the past.

"I hope she likes the gift I got for her," she muttered, trying to decide on the right color for the tablecloth. "I hear she likes red gems very much. I hope her tastes haven't changed."

Mary did like red gems. Ethen had also given her such gems from time to time. It was the only thing he had known about her preferences since he'd taken so little interest in her.

"I think something else might be better," Ethen mumbled.

"Huh?" The duchess looked up at her son.

"Oh, she hasn't seemed very interested in gems lately..." Ethen explained. Mary hadn't seemed all that impressed when he gave her the ruby ring. She'd liked gifts other than gems or clothing more, as if her interests had changed.

"Is that so? Maybe I should prepare something else, then. I can't send her home empty-handed. We haven't met for years." The duchess looked at her son. "What do you think she'll like?"

She seemed to want a definite answer. Ethen thought for a moment.

A present that made Mary happy... She'd seemed happy when he gave her tickets to Lady Priscilla's performance and when he'd told her he could lend her the voice recorder. *What else had pleased her?* A scene floated into his mind.

"Here. We can each keep one to remind us of today."

Ethen recalled the way Mary had handed him the black teddy bear. She'd seemed more excited than usual, perhaps because of the mood of the festival or because she'd wanted to forget something that had been on her mind.

"Lord Ethen, you hit twice as many targets in one game as I did in three. That was incredible."

Mary had walked ahead with a white teddy bear, the same as the one he was holding except for its color. And she'd worn a perfectly contented smile on her face—one he'd never seen from her before.

"Ethen?"

He blushed as he recalled the day of the festival. "I think she prefers something meaningful... over luxury items," he said, belatedly pulling himself together and trying not to show his discomfiture. But his face was already as red as it could be, and the duchess found this extremely cute.

"I see. Something meaningful..." She suddenly remembered a strange teddy bear in Ethen's room recently. Perhaps that was what he was thinking of. Pretending not to have noticed, she said with a bright smile, "Perhaps I can embroider something for her."

"I'm sure she'll like it."

"In that case, I guess I'll have to think of a design."

She would be busy with the party coming up, but she still had enough time to embroider something. There were only three days to go until the day of the party. An event that

some were excited for and others eager to avoid, each for
their own reasons.

CHAPTER
ONE HUNDRED AND EIGHT

The days one wished to avoid always came faster than the others.

I sighed as I looked in the mirror, and Anna, who was doing my hair, seemed greatly disconcerted. She studied me timidly.

"Do you not like it? Shall I try a different style?"

"It's fine. With looks like mine, it doesn't matter how I style my hair," I said, looking at the lovely face in the mirror.

I really was beautiful. Glossy red hair rippled like sea waves under the sunset, and the deep, jewel-like red eyes glittered captivatingly. My skin was like a baby's, my eyes alluring like a cat's, my face small, and my features in perfect harmony.

My face wasn't the problem. Something else was.

"You're going to the duke's mansion, so I suppose you'll be wearing the accessories Lord Ethen bought you?"

"Get those out of my sight."

Anna hid the jewelry box behind her back and smiled awkwardly. The problem was that I was dressing up to visit none other than the duke's mansion. I would have to meet Ethen there no matter what, and he would be escorting me. I didn't know how I could endure meeting with him.

I also have to pretend that nothing is wrong between us. Will I be able to do this?

"H-how about these, then? The master brought them back from his recent business trip…"

"That one will do," I said, nodding without even looking at it properly.

Realizing that I was upset about something, Anna quietly put the necklace and earrings on me. When she was done, an undeniably beautiful woman was gazing back at me from the mirror with a glum look on her face.

"I'm sure he'll have eyes for no one but you," Anna said timorously. She probably said it to make me feel better, but I just wanted to stay out of sight while I was there.

"Yes, of course."

I knew better than anyone that it wasn't likely to happen. I was the duke's future daughter-in-law, and there was no way I could avoid attracting attention at the duchess' party.

"It's tiring, but what can I do about it? Such is my fate."

Yes. It can't be helped. It was something I would have to put up with as long as I remained Mary Bell.

"What about Aria?"

"Lady Aria should be almost done, my lady." Anna got up and turned toward the door as if to check on Aria right away.

"All right. We should leave soon."

I should do my best to act normally and wait for the party to end. I got up and walked toward the door.

"Please don't cause any trouble today, all right? I'm begging you," May said.

"I've never caused trouble. What are you talking about?"

Staying out of trouble was exactly what I wanted. Agreeing with him inwardly, I turned my head away.

May sounded baffled as he replied, "What? You don't remember?"

"Remember what?"

"What you did the last time you met the duchess?"

How am I supposed to know that? I wasn't Mary Bell back then. I shrugged at him.

"Ha! You don't remember it?" May said, barking a laugh of disbelief.

What do you expect me to say? I really have no idea. "What did I do?"

"You—" May cut himself short with an uncomfortable glance at Aria.

Hey, don't stop there! That is so annoying! I glared at him.

"If you're going to say it, say it. Otherwise, don't bother to mention it at all. What the hell is this?"

May quivered angrily, clenching his teeth. He seemed to be holding himself back. "I'll have you know... I'm only being nice because Lady Aria is here with us."

"Aria doesn't care about that sort of thing. Isn't that right, Aria?"

"What? Yes, of course," she responded with a smile, unaware of what this was about.

"Is that right? So, you really want me to say it?"

"Yes, say it. I'm starting to doubt if you're actually capable of saying it."

A vein popped out on May's forehead. Glowering at me with eyes laden with meaning, he said quietly, "Well, you do make trouble so often, it's not surprising you've forgotten."

"What?"

"I'll tell you what happened that day," May said solemnly, which was extremely unlike him.

Up until that point, I had been staring out the window with little concern, watching the scenery, but what he said next made me stiffen with shock.

"You grabbed the hair of another lady at a party hosted by the duchess."

"I did?"

Quickly poring over my memories, I recalled a certain segment of the novel. A description of Mary Bell's misdeeds had included an incident like that. *I knew about that, but...*

"At a party hosted by the duchess?" I asked.

"Yes. Do you know how much you pissed off the duchess... Ahem." With a glance at Aria, he stopped and cleared his throat. "In any case, this is the first time she's invited you to anything since that day. She used to care for you a lot, you know, but she all but cut ties with you for years..."

He didn't have to say much more for me to guess what the duchess must have thought of Mary after that.

"Think of this as an opportunity to repair your relationship with her. You need to make a good impression, all right?"

She probably hated Mary with a passion. I would have felt the same. She'd been good to Mary because she was her son's fiancée, but all she had done was smear her reputation at her own party. Mary probably hadn't even apologized after that.

"Why... why did Mary do such a thing?" Aria stammered. She seemed to be astounded to hear it as well.

May glanced cautiously in my direction. "She spoke ill of Mary behind her back. Mary got angry after she heard about it, and she was too young to know that she shouldn't act so rash—"

"Oh, so that's what it was." Aria cut May off in a relieved tone, smiling.

"I'm... sorry?" May blinked, trying to understand her reaction.

I was just as taken aback. I'd expected her to be shocked or disappointed in me. "Uhm... well..."

"Still, Mary, violence is never a good thing. Even if you were offended, you shouldn't have done such a thing in public," Aria chastised, but then May, who was back to his senses, defended me for some reason.

"Oh, but that was a long time ago. She was scolded heavily by our parents, and she never repeated that mistake again."

"Really?" Aria asked.

"Of course. I'm no longer a child, Aria," I said hurriedly.

She took my hand. "Promise me you won't ever do that again."

"What am I, a baby?" I asked, flustered.

She shook my hand as if pressing me for an answer.

"I wouldn't do such a thing. What kind of person do you think I am?" I said glumly, and Aria laughed as she let go of my hand.

Why is she being like this? Like she's my mother or something...

I turned toward the window, confused to be scolded for something from several years ago that I hadn't even done. The carriage sped on toward our destination as an awkward silence fell.

"We've arrived."

The carriage stopped in front of the duke's mansion. I hadn't visited this place since Ethen, and I had agreed to a month's reprieve. I would be lying if I said I didn't mind going inside.

But I couldn't let my feelings show or refuse to enter. Taking a deep breath, I stepped out of the carriage.

"Welcome, my lady." The servants of the mansion were waiting for us outside. "Please come with us. We'll guide you in," said an old steward.

Aria, May, and I walked behind him, but the steward seemed perturbed by this.

"Lady Mary Bell should come with me. But the maid will guide the two of you."

"Why?" Aria asked, bewildered.

"Lady Mary must enter with Lord Ethen. You may enter the party venue right away, my lady, my lord."

I have to enter with Ethen? I didn't expect this. I quickly looked at the two of them, and they nodded and followed the maid.

"See you later, Mary." Aria waved to me with a disappointed look on her face.

No. Please stay. If you two leave, I have to meet Ethen by myself. I would choke from the awkwardness... I stared pleadingly at them, but that changed nothing.

"This way, my lady." The steward pressed me onward.

I hate this. I would give anything not to go, I repeated in my brain as I walked behind him.

"Is the duchess with him?" I asked.

"She is already at the party, greeting the guests. You two will be the stars of the party, after all," the steward said.

From the moment I learned of what I'd done the last time I met the duchess; I'd been as unwilling to meet her as I was Ethen. But meeting her as well would have been better than meeting Ethen alone. I lamented as I quietly sighed.

"The duchess has put in a lot of effort for this party, saying she hadn't invited you in a while."

"She really didn't have to..."

"It was necessary. You will be part of the family one day."

Part of the family. The words pricked at my conscience.

I had been invited despite all the trouble I'd caused—because I was Ethen's fiancée. They were being forgiving because of that. But I had no intention of marrying Ethen. I wondered if it was all right for me to accept such kindness.

Perhaps they would feel betrayed once they learned that things had ended between me and Ethen. The duchess had forgotten my offense from years ago, and this was her way of showing me forgiveness...

"Just two weeks to go..."

"I beg your pardon?"

"Oh, it's nothing. Just show me the way," I muttered quietly, then clamped my eyes shut for a moment. I would be rubbing salt in her wound. What was more, I'd learned about what I had done only today, and that made me feel worse.

Hanging my head, I walked on behind the steward. Feelings of remorse, coupled with the thought that it couldn't be helped, tortured my mind.

"Ah!" As I walked with my head down, I collided with something. It didn't hurt enough for it to have been a wall. Rubbing my forehead, I looked up.

"Are you all right?"

A nervous-looking Ethen was standing in front of me in a suit, studying my forehead.

ONE HUNDRED AND NINE

Ethen looked down at me worriedly as I rubbed my forehead. He extended a hand.

"I'm fine," I said, backing away quickly before his large, warm hand could touch my forehead. Unable to look him in the eye, I stared at the floor again. "I was just lost in thought. My apologies."

"It's fine. But your hair..." Ethen cautiously stroked my hair, which had become tangled while I was rubbing my forehead.

"I said I'm fine." My voice sounded irritated this time.

Ethen glanced at me timidly, pulling his hand back and standing in an awkward pose. "Well, it's been quite a while, Lady Mary."

"Yes, it's been a while," I said uncomfortably, still unable to look at him. I couldn't see his expression, but I doubted he was smiling.

"You... look beautiful today," he said quietly after a pause. It was a simple comment, but I felt certain he had put a lot of thought into it. I bit my lip.

"I couldn't come looking like a tramp to a party held at your mansion."

"Still... you're always beautiful, but you seem even prettier than usual today. Perhaps it's because we haven't met in a while," he said softly.

The affection in his voice made me uncomfortable. Repressing the urge to run away, I said, "I was surprised by the sudden invitation. And I heard that the duke wanted to hold an engagement ceremony for us this year."

"He probably wants to hurry things along because he doesn't know about our agreement," said Ethen.

I had known this, of course—Ethen wasn't the sort to go back on his word. And he definitely would not have used such an underhanded method to keep me from leaving him.

"In return for delaying the ceremony, my parents wanted to show off our relationship to the public. I couldn't find an excuse to stop them from doing that."

"I understand. But this will make things even more difficult two weeks from now," I said, reminding him that nothing would change about our relationship in that time. I wouldn't be changing my mind, so I needed to prepare for what would happen after we became completely estranged.

I would be rudely insulting the duchess once more, and the public would be taken aback by the sudden announcement. I could do neither of those things without a prick of conscience or a shade of embarrassment.

"Don't worry about that," Ethen said, looking down at me.

I finally lifted my head to face him and blinked at him dumbly.

"People will think that our relationship ended because of me."

"You're kidding, right?" I asked, frowning.

Though I knew that my parents, the duchess, and various other people would point accusatory fingers at me, I intended for the cause to be my fickleness, nothing more. Everyone knew that Mary Bell was capricious and wayward. The engagement had to end on my account, either through a fault of my own or because I had a change of heart. My reputation was far from stellar, and doing so would be the better choice. The shock was probably immense for Ethen as things stood. I didn't want to burden him any further.

"I mean it. That way, I can keep my father and mother from resenting you."

"You don't need to worry about that. Does that mean you don't care if my parents end up disliking you, then?" I asked with a rigid expression. I had no intention of making Ethen suffer any further.

"I know that your reputation will suffer even if I'm the one calling this off, but at least there will be no direct damage to you." He seemed resigned to any unpleasant consequences that might result for him.

I laughed in disbelief. "I never asked you to do that."

"I'm sorry?" Ethen asked, puzzled by my aggressive response.

"When did I ever ask you to do such a thing? All I asked was to call things off and for you to give up on changing my mind after a month had passed. That's all."

In reality, I wanted even less from him. The only thing I wanted from him now was that he would stop loving me. But that wish was never going to be fulfilled, so I had chosen to stay away from him instead.

"I don't wish for anything else from you. You're making decisions on your own and burdening yourself with the consequences. Did you think that would please me?"

"Lady Mary."

"No. Not at all. I don't like it in the least. Did you think I couldn't handle something like that?"

Perhaps I could avoid being a villainess, but I seemed fated to hurt Ethen in the end. Maybe that was impossible to change, no matter how much I shifted the future and the plot.

"I don't want that kind of consideration from you." I glared at him. He seemed confused by my reaction because he was looking at me with a strange expression.

"I'm not trying to come off as condescending. You're a strong woman. I don't doubt that you could handle it." Ethen looked at my lips as I bit down on them. "But even if you could, even if it was something so small that it would hardly make you bat an eye... I would like to keep you from experiencing it if I could. That is the only reason I'm planning to do things this way."

What is this foolish man thinking? Why would he sacrifice his own reputation to protect me? I've never done him any good. In truth, I'd been nothing but trouble to him. *Why does he care so much about me?*

"That's none of your concern. I can handle my own affairs. I will take responsibility for my own choices, so don't even think of trying to deal with everything by yourself." I turned away from him. If this conversation went on any longer, I felt like my emotions would burst and I would start crying like an idiot.

"Anyway," I said, "I hope I've made myself clear. I'm the one who suggested calling off this marriage, so when the month is over, I will be the one sending notice to your house. Don't confuse the duke or the duchess by suggesting anything to the contrary." I rattled off the words without looking at him. "Let's go now. The party must have started a while ago. They'll think it strange if we don't show up soon." I started walking without even knowing the way to the venue.

"Wait. Let me show you the way," Ethen said, finally recovering his composure and walking in front of me.

He looked so good today, as usual. Everything from his hair to his clothing, his cuff buttons, even his shoes showed signs of the effort he'd gone to so that he could look good. It was all wasted effort. *Why did he have to show up looking so handsome and make me feel upset?*

With a quiet sigh, I followed him.

We walked into the garden arm in arm.

"Oh my, Lady Mary! It's been so long," the duchess said, walking over with a smile.

Because Ethen was the spitting image of the duke, I'd expected him to bear no resemblance to his mother. But the similarity was there. It was so clear that I could tell at a glance that they were mother and son.

"Happy to meet you again, Duchess Frangert. I hope you've been well."

"Of course. I should have invited you here more often, but I've been too busy. I'm sorry about that," the duchess said.

I ignored the fact that it hadn't been because she was busy but because she despised me, and I smiled back at her.

"Oh, you don't need to apologize about that. You know I wouldn't be upset about such a thing," I said, leaning on Ethen's arm and covering my mouth.

People began to whisper among themselves when they saw us having a pleasant conversation.

"Oh my! I thought the duchess disliked Lady Mary. That doesn't seem to be the case, does it?"

"Well, she probably isn't angry at her anymore. Besides, Lady Mary has been showing pretty good behavior of late, hasn't she?"

I ignored the murmuring and smiled confidently at the duchess. "It must have been hard to find all these roses in the garden. They aren't even in season."

"I had them specially prepared for you since you like roses. Do you like them?"

I glanced around. There were roses everywhere. I picked one up from the table. "Of course. I'm so touched by your warm welcome."

"My goodness, you are even more beautiful than that rose!" the duchess joked, looking at me and the rose in my hand.

"Oh, I'm far more fragrant and beautiful than this flower," I said without skipping a beat. I looked up at Ethen. "Don't you agree?"

Despite the uncomfortable situation, I had to play my part to perfection today. I forced myself to smile at him.

"Of course, Lady Mary," Ethen said, smiling back and taking the rose as if he had no concerns at all. "This flower can't compare to someone like you." He smiled as he gave me the embarrassing compliment and put the flower back in the vase.

Those who heard him were making a fuss.

"Goodness gracious, did you hear him just now?"

"To think the reticent Lord Ethen would say such a thing!"

"I guess the rumors are right about him being in love with her."

Perhaps this would satisfy the duke's desire to show off my relationship with Ethen.

Stifling a sigh, I said, "Yes. There are many flowers, but I'm one of a kind."

"Hahaha! Of course. Oh, Lady Mary," the duchess said. She gestured to a maid, who brought over a small box. "This is a welcome gift I prepared for you, as we haven't seen each other for so long. Will you accept it?"

"Oh my. I'm very curious to see what it is," I responded mechanically as I took it from her. The box was small, which meant it was probably earrings, a necklace, or a ring.

"Haha. I took my son's advice when preparing this."

Then it's probably something with a ruby. I undid the ribbon and opened the lid, not anticipating much.

But to my surprise, the object in the box was nothing like jewelry.

CHAPTER
ONE HUNDRED AND TEN

The object in the box was a handkerchief.

Bewildered, I looked at the duchess.

She laughed. "I considered a lot of different gifts, but something meaningful is always best, right?"

"Does that mean…" I said, rubbing the rose-shaped embroidery on one corner of the handkerchief.

"Yes," the duchess immediately replied. "I embroidered it myself as a token of my best wishes. Please make good use of it."

I realized I would have preferred something like gems much more. Feeling uncomfortable, I closed the box and forced myself to smile. "Thank you. It's such a heartwarming gift. I think I'll remember it for a long time."

"Ethen gave me some advice on what to prepare. I'm happy that you like it," she said, covering her mouth and laughing.

"Oh my. Really? Thank you, Lord Ethen." I looked up at him, keeping up the unnatural smile. I had to act like everything was fine between us, at least for today.

"They make such a lovely couple."

"Lord Ethen must care for her very much. I mean, I noticed it at the hunting competition as well, but his every action shows how much he cares for her."

People were complimenting Ethen's manners and our relationship. And it wasn't only strangers speaking this way.

"Mary," Aria said, a proud look on her face as she approached us.

"Oh my. Who is this?" the duchess asked.

"My name is Aria Peridot. I've been staying with Lady Mary as her guest," Aria said, bowing politely to the duchess.

May, who had come with her, also bowed with a slightly nervous look. "It's been such a long time, Duchess."

"Lord May. I trust you've been well?" May's anxiety aside, the duchess welcomed him as if she'd been eager to see him and held out her hand. "I'm very honored to be able to invite the marquess' children to my party. Not that you'll need an invitation to come here much longer," she said, referring to the marriage she assumed would happen soon. "So, you're the singer everyone's been talking about. Nice to meet you."

"It is such an honor to meet you," Aria replied.

"Haha! Perhaps I could ask you to sing a song for a certain special day."

It seemed the duchess couldn't speak more than a few sentences without making another reference to my marriage to Ethen. I knew that this was in line with the intention of this party, but I couldn't help feeling a prick of guilt each time.

"Are you feeling well?" Ethen asked worriedly, seeing me look exhausted after only a few minutes.

"I'm fine. You don't have to worry about me." I smiled like nothing was wrong. I was far from fine, but what else could I say when the duchess was looking right at me?

"Lady Mary!"

Ashley and Maia were walking over from some distance away. I hadn't met with them at all recently, so I wondered how they managed to look so happy to see me each time.

I'd thought them to be opportunists, looking to gain something from Mary's wealth, but I realized that I'd been wrong about them. They were so kind-hearted as to be foolish and blindly devoted to Mary.

"So, your friends are here, too," Ethen said, glancing at the two of them then smiling at me. "It must have been a while since you've seen them. You'll need time to speak with them as well." He removed my arm from his.

Surprised, I blinked up at him. "Are you sure you won't mind?"

"Of course."

I found it uncomfortable being with him, of course, but I'd still intended to stick by his side out of duty. I hadn't expected him to show such consideration.

Taking an awkward step away from him, I said, "Well... I won't refuse." I couldn't thank him because that would imply that I wanted to get away from him.

"Lady Mary, we were worried because you went home in such a hurry after the hunting competition. Are you feeling all right?"

"I'm fine. You don't have to worry about me," I said, waving to the fussing Ashley.

We walked away casually. *I suppose going somewhere out of sight of Ethen will help me calm down.*

Nudging them toward a corner, I said, "It's too bad I missed the parade, but it couldn't be helped. My health matters more."

"You're right," Maia said with a laugh, unaware of the real reason I'd left the way I did.

Now that we were some distance away from the duchess and Ethen, I finally sighed and relaxed.

"Nice to see you as well, Lady Aria."

"She and I met recently," Ashley said.

What? I looked up in shock at Ashley's words. "You met?"

"Ah, yes."

I looked at Ashley and Aria with a suspicious expression. I couldn't think of a single reason for them to meet on their own.

"Lady Ashley, if you'll excuse m—"

"I saw her walking out of a dressmaker's shop," Ashley said before Aria could stop her. "I spoke to her, thinking she was with you, Lady Mary, but she was with someone else instead."

"Who?" I hadn't been able to do anything to learn about what Aria had been up to. I didn't think I would hear about it like this. I was almost glaring now. "Tell me when and where, and who she was with. All the details."

"W-wait, this is rather sudden..." Ashley backed away and glanced nervously over at me. She seemed to cast her mind back for a moment. "I think it was four days ago. It was a dressmaker's shop downtown, and it wasn't Madam Rosalie's shop."

"Who was she with? Do you know?"

"I didn't get a good look at her... All I remember is that she was neatly dressed," Ashley said, weakly grabbing at her hair as if in frustration.

So, Aria met a woman. Who could it be?

"And it wasn't Lady Iris?"

"If it was, I'd have recognized her. It wasn't her."

If she was neatly dressed, it had to be a noble or a member of the upper class, at least. I tried to think of an upper-class woman Aria might have met but came up empty.

"As I said, I'll tell you when the time comes," Aria said with a mischievous smile. She seemed to relax after hearing Ashley's vague information.

"Don't be silly. I'll die of old age while I wait," I said, pouting.

"Oh my, you're all here." Iris came toward us as if on cue.

"Lady Iris. It's been a while."

Though Ashley said otherwise, I wasn't convinced that it hadn't been Iris that Aria had been secretly meeting. I decided to sound her out.

"So, have you been enjoying the party?" I asked.

"It's obvious how much care the duchess has put into the preparations for your sake, Lady Mary. She must care a lot about you." She gave the cutest, most kind-hearted smile I'd ever seen. It was as if her vicious behavior on the first day we met had been a dream. "I know you'll be family soon, but it's as if she already thinks of you that way. That was nice to see."

"Well... of course. We'll be family soon enough," I said with an awkward laugh.

Iris turned to Aria. "Lady Aria, I trust you've been well, too?"

"Oh, of course. How about you, Lady Iris?"

The two fell into a genial conversation.

"Did you know that the dessert shop we went to last time has put out a new cake?"

"Ah, yes. I went once after that because I remembered how nice the food was. They had citron cake. That wasn't something I'd seen before, so I tried it out."

The dessert shop? They went to the dessert shop together? I pretended to be uninterested, but my ears pricked up.

"Really? Did it taste good?"

"Yes. I heard that it became popular the moment it was released. I could tell why. It was delicious—sweet and sour at the same time."

I did my best to detect clues from this mundane conversation.

"Nothing like sweets to do away with stress, huh?"

"Haha. You're right! But sometimes you get a hankering for sweet food even when you're not frustrated over something."

Frustrated? What was she frustrated about?

"Besides, it wasn't just the food that was great that day. I loved the conversation even more."

"Oh my. How nice of you to say that. Call for me anytime if you need a willing ear. I'm all for conversations like that."

When did they become so close? Although I was facing Ashley and Maia, my attention was focused solely on the conversation behind me.

A moment later, I was startled when Ashley called me. "Lady Mary, you'll do that, right?"

"Huh? What?" I was forced to pay attention to the two ladies in front of me again. "What were we talking about?"

"Oh, Lady Mary. We were asking for two of the best seats at Lady Aria's first performance," Maia said chidingly.

"We'd like to watch from good seats," Ashley said, pouting.

It wasn't a difficult request, but I had no idea what part Aria would be performing in the coming imperial troupe performance, which prevented me from agreeing right away.

"Well, if you're patient, maybe you'll hear some good news from me."

I'll do my best, but please be aware that I might not be able to accommodate you.

"I'm so excited."

"So am I."

Their eyes were shining as they looked at me. I appreciated how friendly they were being, but I really needed to focus elsewhere. After hurriedly calming Ashley and Maia down, I looked around for Aria and Iris.

"That's why I've brought someone special to meet you today," Iris said in a low, suggestive tone.

I stiffened, forgetting for a moment that I was eavesdropping on their conversation. *Someone special? Aria doesn't have anyone like that.*

That wasn't the only reason I was dumbfounded. Iris' innocent expression was gone. Instead, the malicious look on her face reminded me of the first time I'd met her.

"You said you and your father were close."

"I'm... sorry?" Aria said, looking as confused as I was.

"I noticed how much you cared about your father. So, I brought him here."

I heard Iris' words, but I couldn't believe my ears.

CHAPTER ONE HUNDRED AND ELEVEN

"What nonsense is this?" Completely shocked, I went over to Iris, forgetting the fact that I'd been eavesdropping. But someone else got to Aria first.

"Well now, it certainly has been a while, Aria."

I'd never met the man in person, but I immediately recognized him. He had Aria's hair and eyes. Although he was a mess from leading a dissolute lifestyle, there was no doubt he had been handsome in his youth.

"Father..."

This was obviously Edward Peridot, Aria's father.

There was a murmur from those who had taken notice of him.

"Viscount Peridot?"

"I don't think I've ever seen him in high society before..."

"Oh my. But the same could be said of Lady Aria, don't you think? No one knew of her until a few months ago."

At this rate, he'll do something that will ruin Aria's reputation. I walked over to Aria without hesitation. "Aria."

"Ah, you must be the marquess' daughter Aria has been staying with. I couldn't help but recognize you, given how striking your looks are," Edward said unctuously.

He wore clean clothes, which contrasted with his rude behavior and pale face, making for an odd display. There was no way a drunkard like him had enough money to buy such clothing. It was clear he'd had help. And it wasn't difficult to guess where this help had come from.

"You said you felt apologetic toward your father. Well, conversation is the only way to deal with such problems, is it not?" Lady Iris was smiling, but I couldn't have felt more disgusted. I stared at her with a stone-cold expression as she grinned, pretending to mean well.

"Lady Iris, that's not—"

"You said you once wished your father would disappear. But you only said that because you still love him, right?" Iris continued with the grin still on her face, shocking the crowd.

Aria had wished that her father would disappear. Such a statement was not at all acceptable by the empire's social standards, so, predictably, people started speaking ill of her.

"What? She wished her father would disappear?"

"How could she think that about her own father? I thought she was a kind soul, even though she comes from a poor background…"

"You know better than I do that's not what I meant," Aria said, her voice trembling slightly. I wondered if it was Edward's appearance that had shaken her or the fact that Iris had been secretly planning this all along despite her mask of kindness.

Perhaps it's both. I approached Aria to calm her down. "You don't need to explain yourself to her."

"That's right. I doubt Lady Aria really meant that she wanted her father to disappear. She couldn't have!" Iris said with a cruel smile.

Edward, who'd been listening, suddenly began making a fuss. "Is that what you thought of me? That breaks my heart!"

Liar. You don't look heartbroken at all. I stared angrily at Edward as he feigned hurt.

"I'll admit, I wasn't as good of a father to you as I should have been after your mother died of her illness. It wasn't easy looking after you…" he said, trying his best to squeeze tears from his eyes. Given his obvious skill in acting, I wondered why he wasn't working with some theatrical troupe. "Still, you must know how much I love you in my heart."

"Oh, my goodness…"

Onlookers watched this farce with concern, apparently unaware of his deceit. In this situation, I didn't think explaining that he was a leech who'd depended on his daughter to feed him all his life would improve the mood much. It might even have the opposite effect—people might have thought I was lying to get Aria out of her straits.

"Lady Aria, a conversation is where healing starts. If you tell your father the things you told me, about the ways you felt hurt by him, I'm sure the viscount will understand," Iris said, pretending to want what was best for her.

How long has she been plotting something like this? I bit my lip and glared at Edward.

"Aaaah!"

After the tea party at the imperial palace was over, Iris had returned to her mansion. She'd screamed as she threw her fan down on the bed.

"Well, we've never mentioned this so far, but... Lady Aria has never done us any harm. What right do we have to meddle in Lady Mary's friendships?"

"That's right. I understand that you don't like Lady Aria because Lady Mary rebuked you in public, Lady Iris... but that wasn't Lady Aria's fault, was it?"

Never done us any harm? Meddle? To think that irritating girl had done nothing wrong!

It was clear that everyone was being fooled.

"Lady Mary was never that generous with anybody. That nasty girl must have done something..." Iris muttered, chewing her nails.

Lady Mary Bell was the woman Iris had admired most, a person she'd wanted to speak with, even for a short while, even if Lady Mary was cold to her.

That was what she had always thought of Mary. She was rude, cold, and completely reckless, but everyone seemed to be cautious around her. Lady Mary was the perfect example of a high-society queen. No matter how rude she might be, she never looked bad in Iris' eyes. This had been true even when Mary had poured wine over Iris' clothing.

I suppose I did bother her a little too much.

Though it had obviously been Mary's fault, Iris had blamed herself for the incident, as she always did. This was the way she had always behaved, at least until she heard a certain piece of news.

"Impossible."

Iris had gone down with a terrible cold, of all things, during the birthday celebration period, and she was not able to participate. But when a close friend told her what had happened at the celebration, she doubted her ears.

"I mean it. Lady Mary's clothing was a mess, but she didn't grab the girl's hair or throw wine in her face. Instead, she gave the girl a gift. How lucky is she?"

Who is this girl that is given such special treatment? Iris hadn't been able to get the tiniest bit of interest from Lady Mary, even after all her efforts.

"Oh, surely Lady Mary was just being nice because it was the emperor's birthday..."

"That's what I thought as well, but I've been told that Lady Mary actually gave the girl a dress."

Iris bit her lip. Iris was merely the daughter of a count, hardly influential compared to Lady Mary, but her family was still well-reputed. She believed she was qualified to be Mary's friend, albeit not as much as Lady Ashley or Lady Maia, with their close connections to the marquess' house.

But someone had taken the spot of Mary's closest friend—not Iris, not the daughter of a powerful house, but a wretched girl from an unknown family.

"Iris, people will create friendships with others of their caliber. The people you spend your time with will be a testament to your status."

"If you can't even please a marquess' daughter, how will you accomplish anything in life?" Iris recalled the words of her parents.

I did my best. I tried to become someone worthy of Lady Mary's friendship to please my parents...

"My goodness, who would have thought that Lady Mary would actually find a lady she liked?"

So why is it that someone else is taking the place that should be mine?

At first, she was unable to bear the frustration and questioned Mary about it. Mary had behaved as she usually did toward Iris while being kind to the viscount's daughter once again. And after seeing this with her own eyes, Iris' rage shifted its target to Aria.

That girl must have Lady Mary under her spell. I need to find out what use Lady Mary has for such a nondescript lady. Then Lady Mary will see her mistake and thank me.

Her misdirected anger grew and grew, but Aria Peridot seemed to be completely clean. There was nothing to malign her with other than her lackluster background.

"She must be extremely clever. How else could someone like her have won Lady Mary over?" Iris had repeated these words to herself without end, but when she heard that Mary planned to turn Aria into a singer, she finally realized what it was.

That's it. Lady Mary has no interest in music. She must think anyone with a pretty voice is a good singer. My goodness, does this mean the girl got all Lady Mary's affections with her boring singing skills?

Iris secretly mocked Aria. *She'll make a fool of herself soon enough. And then everything will return to normal.*

But she had been wrong. Aria really had an excellent voice, and Iris herself had to admit it.

"But I suppose merely having a good voice can't be enough to attract Lady Mary. She must have pulled something tricky."

However, that did not mean that Iris could accept that Aria occupied the position she currently did. Iris believed that Lady Mary and the others had to learn that the girl was not all that she was made out to be. She'd spent her days with such thoughts in her head, but she was merely treated like an idle meddler.

An idle meddler? How could I be such a thing? Everyone will learn before long. They'll see that I was right when they see her for what she is.

After a considerable amount of time had passed, Iris was told an intriguing bit of news.

"I hear the Church Angel is performing on the streets."

"Sarah has the day off, and she's going to see her. I'm so envious."

It was by pure chance that she had overheard the maids talking.

"You there. Get over here."

"Yes, my lady?"

"By Church Angel, do you mean Lady Aria?"

After questioning the maids, Iris learned that Aria was indeed performing on the streets. She put on some casual clothing and went out to see for herself.

"I can't see a damn thing. How annoying…"

Commoners had been waiting for a while for the performance to start, and she couldn't find herself a spot close to Aria.

"Well, this is what street performances are like. Poor experiences all around." Irritated, Iris decided to go back to her mansion, when a knight wearing a hood walked past her and commanded his subordinates to drag someone out.

"Get him."

Moments later, Aria suddenly stopped singing, and the crowd began to murmur.

"Huh? Why isn't she singing?"

"Let go of me, you bastards! You know who I am? Huh?"

In the confusion, the crowd had been staring worriedly at Aria, who had gone silent, but Iris' eyes were locked on the man who was being pulled away.

CHAPTER
ONE HUNDRED AND TWELVE

"Let go of me! Do you know who I am? Ugh! Mmf!"

The knights dragged the man away, clamping a hand over his mouth. The man looked very similar to the woman Iris hated most in the world.

He looked like a drunkard on the street, but something seemed to suggest there was more to him. The man had the same color hair and eyes as the woman, and though he had dark circles under his eyes, probably from constant drinking, upon close inspection his face resembled hers. If the stupid look was erased and his eyes were livelier, he could look a lot like Aria.

"Pern," Iris said to one of her guards.

"Yes, my lady."

"Go after the man the knights just dragged away and bring him to me. Tell him I have something to discuss about his daughter."

That's right, not much is known about Viscount Peridot. Perhaps this is a chance to expose her for who she is.

Iris smiled at the thought.

"Who are you, exactly? What do you want with me? I thought you were that lady from the House of Bell, damn it!"

The rudeness apparent in every word he said grated on Iris, but she was willing to put up with it if it meant getting rid of both father and daughter in one fell swoop.

"I heard you've been wronged."

Before bringing Edward to the mansion, Iris had sent her men to the house where Aria used to live to scout out the situation.

"My goodness," she said with a sad look on her face. "To think she abandoned her father and went to live a life of luxury in the marquess' mansion by herself... How could a daughter do that to her father?"

"Finally! Someone recognizes my plight. That's exactly what I've been saying," Edward shouted, his face red with agitation. "I raised her, and now she can make money on her own. That means she should be bringing that money to me. Now that she's grown a bit more capable, she's completely abandoned me..."

Edward had been going around saying the same thing to the villagers, but no one had sympathized with him—if anything, he'd been disdained. But a lady who lived in a luxurious mansion had appeared out of the blue and was obviously empathetic. This was great news for him.

"None of the commoner idiots seemed to understand, but I can see that you're a woman of culture. My lady, I believe we are on the same page."

"Haha. It must have been difficult, Viscount, living among foolish commoners like that."

Edward raised his chin in the air in satisfaction at the word "viscount." Though he looked like a pauper, he was still Viscount Peridot. He was different from the commoners, but no one had recognized that. No one had treated him like a noble for a long time. He ran his hand through his hair, suddenly in a great mood.

"I'm honored that you recognize my status."

Iris sighed with relief as she gazed at Edward's stupid face. *He'll do whatever I ask if I praise him a little.*

"Lady Mary takes such good care of Lady Aria," she said, "but she doesn't spare a single glance for you, her father... You must have felt so upset." Iris made a commiserating face, as if she was the one who felt wronged, not Edward.

"She's been plying Aria with false hopes, promising she can be a singer and whatnot. Honestly, I'll be relieved if all this doesn't ruin her chances of marrying a nice man. And she should have paid me money to take Aria away, seeing as she's the breadwinner. But no—"

"I've heard about your situation, Viscount. You've been prohibited from enjoying your hobby, and you're not allowed any credit in the village—am I right?"

Mary had been incredibly firm with Edward, according to the information Iris had heard from her men. She had bought out the shops in the village to keep Viscount Peridot from making luxurious purchases in Aria's name. Not only that, but she had also sent people to the gambling houses to prevent him from going anywhere near them. It seemed Lady Mary was very serious about keeping Edward at bay.

"But I've heard that she's been giving you some allowances in return..."

"Oh, yes, but who knows when that will stop? I tried to embarrass her and ask her for more money. But she threatened me instead..."

You tried to embarrass her? Iris was elated. This was precisely what Iris had been planning to make Edward do.

If their goal was the same, then it would be easy to buy him off. Trying to hide the excitement in her voice, Iris said, "Let me make you an offer."

After that, Iris paid Edward's living expenses as well as pocket money for entertainment.

"How can a man like you, with a title, do work that's only fit for commoners? We nobles should be helping each other out."

The more she learned about Edward, the more convinced she became that he was an utter idiot. As soon as he got his hands on money he didn't deserve, he began to eat luxury meals and purchase clothes he couldn't afford. Iris was amused that he seemed to think a jacket could somehow boost his status, but she didn't let it show and supported everything he did.

"So, you mean to say that you'll try to find out how she really feels about me?"

"Who knows? Lady Aria might feel a shred of remorse toward you. In that case, we'll be able to reach a pleasant agreement," Iris said, although that wasn't her intention. She couldn't care less what Aria thought of Edward. "I've been planning to speak with Lady Aria myself, you see. I think I'll be able to hear her honest thoughts if we become friends."

"Well, if she were a grateful person, she wouldn't have acted the way she did... but feel free to ask," Edward said, chewing on some fruit that had been set out in the reception room.

How uncivilized, talking with your mouth full. Iris frowned, turning her face away so he couldn't see.

"The hunting competition will be happening soon, so it won't be difficult for me to meet her. Do you have anything you'd like me to tell her?"

"Anything I want you to tell her?" Edward chewed on the fruit and considered her question for a moment. "Well, I want to know where she's hidden her money, if she has any."

Iris smiled at his vulgar reply. It seemed things would go just the way she wanted them to.

"I never said that. But that's precisely why you have a lot to learn. You could insult a lot of people unintentionally."

At the hunting competition, Iris had sided with Aria and criticized Lady Zir. But really, it was Aria she wanted to say these words to.

She is a nuisance to me merely by existing. I wish she would disappear already.

But she needed to keep her intentions hidden for the time being if she was to accomplish her goal. After the situation had been wrapped up somewhat, she approached Aria and consoled her. "Please don't mind what she said."

"Oh, I'm all right," Aria said, smiling shyly. "Besides, you stood up for me today, Lady Iris, like you'd taken personal offense. I don't feel hurt at all because you took my side before I could even start to feel bad."

As Aria thanked Iris, Iris did her best to hide her hostility and act the part of a friendly lady.

"The other ladies don't know that much about you. It's why they're acting the way they are. Even I used to get angry at you for no reason when I didn't know any better."

"Oh, back then..." Aria considered what to say for a moment, studying Iris' expression. She seemed to be wondering how she could avoid blaming Iris for what had happened.

"I'm embarrassed by the way I acted," Iris said.

"No. What matters is now. I'd completely forgotten about that incident. But thank you for your apology."

That day was so humiliating for me. You don't even remember it? Iris did her best not to scowl.

"I was worried the incident was why you didn't take part in the high-society parties."

"Oh, that's not it at all. Mary doesn't like crowded places, so I didn't really feel the need to go, either."

Her statement was even more remarkable than the fact that Aria was on a first-name basis with Lady Mary. *Lady Mary doesn't like crowded places?* That statement was truly absurd.

Iris was annoyed by every word that came from Aria's mouth, but she did her best to seem agreeable. She needed to know Aria through and through if she was to destroy the girl.

"I think you're amazing, Lady Aria."

Iris followed Aria and Mary around on the second day of the hunting competition, trying her best to blend in with them. Mary didn't seem too concerned about anyone that wasn't Aria, and she was often spaced out, thinking about something or other. This allowed Iris to speak with Aria freely.

"You must have learned a lot from Lady Priscilla's performance."

"That's right. I understood the moment I heard the first verse why she's considered the greatest prima donna in the empire," Aria replied, continuing the conversation happily, completely unaware of Iris' intentions.

Iris couldn't understand why Aria seemed so happy or why a performance was such a big deal, but she played along. "I'd love to see a performance with you next time. No, strike that. It's your performance that I'm looking forward to most of all."

"Hahaha! It looks like I'll have to do my best not to disappoint."

Why is she bragging so much? Being a good singer means nothing. Iris feigned interest in music as she conversed with

Aria, but she knew so little about the topic that she quickly ran out of things to say. She smoothly changed the subject.

"You know, I was really surprised at the tea party. Where did you find a dress like that?"

"Oh, Mary ordered it specially from Madam Rosalie. I was surprised when I saw it, too."

"I could tell right away why people have been calling you the Church Angel," Iris said, not meaning a word of what she said.

"I'm no angel, but that dress was worthy of the epithet. Who knew I, a girl with only three dresses in her wardrobe, would end up wearing such a thing?"

Three dresses? She's basically a pauper.

"Only three? Your parents must be very—"

"Ah..."

Iris had been about to say that they must be very frugal, but she realized she'd made a mistake when she saw the look on Aria's face.

CHAPTER ONE HUNDRED AND THIRTEEN

"Your parents must be very—"

"Ah..."

Aria trailed off as Iris mentioned her parents. No doubt the subject wasn't pleasant, given how her mother had passed away early and her father was a rake. Iris knew everything she needed to about Aria's parents already, so she didn't need to say any thoughtless things and ruin Aria's trust.

"Oh my, forgive me. I asked something too personal," Iris said immediately.

"Oh, you don't need to apologize. I—"

"No, I understand. It might not be something you want to talk about." She couldn't afford to ruin the harmless persona she'd built up so far, so she apologized once again. "I'm sorry. I can be like this at times."

Iris seemed to have made the right call. Mary and Aria both looked at her as if they were amazed by how thoughtful she was.

After that conversation, Aria opened up to Iris a little more. Iris' willingness to apologize first and avoid situations where the conversation could grow awkward had its intended effect.

In addition, it proved to be a great thing for Iris that Mary suddenly seemed to be out of her mind after becoming the Lady of the Year, though Iris had no idea why. Mary, who had always annoyingly insisted on having Aria around, locked herself in her room, and it was ridiculously easy for Iris to take advantage of Aria's resulting anxiety. They exchanged a few letters, then Iris suggested they meet at a dessert café because "sweets were the best cure for worries." Aria took the bait easily.

"Did Lady Mary say she was not feeling well today as well?" Iris asked.

"I guess she feels quite unwell. She left abruptly during the hunting competition, and since she returned home, she's had a headache for several days now. I'm worried about her," Aria replied, sipping her drink.

Though Aria was worried about Lady Mary, this was an opportunity for Iris. The more anxious she was, the easier it would be to take advantage. Stifling a scream of delight, she acted concerned for Aria.

"You're right. I'm worried about you as well, Lady Aria."

"M-me?" Aria stammered, pointing at herself.

"Yes. It must have taken a toll on you. You've been worrying about Lady Mary for days, and you look tired too..."

"No, I'm all right." Aria waved her hands in denial, but she didn't seem to dislike Iris' concern. "And the reason I look tired is because I've been preparing something," she said, lowering her head.

"What are you preparing?"

"I've been giving a lot of thought to what I can manage to do alone. Then I came upon this great idea, and I've been working on it in secret ever since... I want it to be a surprise for Mary, and I guess I'm a little exhausted because of that," Aria said with a smile.

What could a girl without money or connections possibly manage? No doubt it's something boring.

"Is it a secret from me as well?"

"Uhm... I think it's best to keep it to myself. I'm sorry."

Iris wasn't interested anyway, so it didn't matter. There were far more important things at hand. She changed the subject.

"It's all right. In fact, I'm looking forward to it. Please be sure to tell me what it is when you're done."

"Yes, I will," Aria said, still smiling.

Iris' plan to win Aria's heart in a short span of time was going wonderfully. She couldn't figure out if the girl was naive or plain stupid. She inwardly mocked Aria for dropping her guard around her.

"You must meet the marchioness often if you live in that mansion," she began, working toward the subject she really wanted to talk about. She wasn't interested in Aria's love for music or her future plans. "Everyone knows Lady Mary's parents love her dearly. How does it feel to see them being so affectionate?"

"Oh, they're usually busy, so I don't see them often, but..." Aria began to talk. "Sometimes, when I see how they treat her, I can understand why Mary is such a kind soul."

Mary, kind? Iris stifled a wry smile and listened.

"I think it's because her parents love her so dearly that she's capable of being so loving to others. She always has this relaxed air about her, you know."

Iris wondered if they were really talking about the same person. The Mary that Iris knew was far from kind. *Relaxed? Perhaps that much is true.* She was so full of confidence that she ignored everyone she met. That wasn't surprising, given her prestigious background and wealth. Therefore, it seemed only right that Mary should treat everyone in the same way.

Iris could not accept that she was giving anyone special treatment, especially when the person was someone as shoddy as Aria.

"Yes. I envy her sometimes," Iris said with a sad look on her face. "My parents have never loved me that way, you see. Oh, I'm sorry. I realize it might be uncomfortable to hear something so personal."

"I-it's all right."

"I've never had anyone to speak about such things with before. It's strange. I feel like I can really open up to you, Lady Aria..."

Aria looked moved by Iris' act and waved her hand in the air. "No, I don't find it uncomfortable at all."

"My parents expect great things from me, but I'm not as great a daughter as they want me to be. It always makes me feel bad."

Though she was saying this with an ulterior motive, she wasn't entirely lying. It was true that Iris hadn't been able to meet her parents' standards when it came to her friends or her abilities.

"My parents probably think I'm useless. That's why I envy Lady Mary for having parents who love her so unconditionally..." Iris squeezed tears from her eyes. "It's natural for parents to love their own children unconditionally. How deficient I must be that not even my own parents trust me! It's all my fault, really."

Aria, who had been listening with a distressed look on her face, said, "Nothing is unconditional."

Though Aria had always been a kind-hearted person, there was another reason she felt so moved by this story. This had been her personal struggle for a very long time, and her heart went out to Iris, who seemed to be experiencing the same thing.

"I thought the same thing as you before, but it's not entirely true," Aria said, holding Iris' hands.

"It's my fault. Not even my own parents think well of me."

"Your parents are only human, just like everyone else, and some people just aren't naturally drawn toward each other. With you, it was your parents. That's all," Aria said with a serious look on her face. She knew she was meddling, but she couldn't ignore Iris' plight.

"You've had such thoughts, too?" Iris asked.

"Yes, I have. I believed it was my fault for failing to satisfy my father. No matter what he did, he was still my father... my precious family." Aria said this while thinking about the last day she saw Edward. "But I'm just as precious as my father is."

Her voice trembled as she harked back to the days when she'd blamed herself for Edward's profligacy. She'd believed that it was all her fault and that something would change if she tried harder. That her father would understand how she felt one day. She was his daughter, after all.

But she now knew that some things never changed, no matter how hard you tried.

"Sometimes, even if you're family, you might only end up hurting each other."

"So, you think I might not be in the wrong?" Iris asked with an innocent look on her face. "I feel so sorry whenever I feel resentful of my parents. I know I wouldn't even exist without them... I'm probably the only person in the world who thinks this way."

"Not at all! Please don't think that way," Aria said, shaking her head. "This is a secret, but I once thought the same thing. I even told myself once that I wished my father would never return."

"Did you ever wish your parents would disappear?"

"I did, yes," Aria said, exaggerating for Iris' sake. She was only trying to console Iris, but this was precisely what Iris had been waiting for.

Iris smiled sincerely at Aria for the first time since she'd met her. "Thank you for saying that. I was actually very anxious."

"Don't blame yourself for everything. That'll make you feel worse."

You sound like such a know-it-all.

Iris answered, "Thank you. I don't know what trouble there is between you and your parents... but I hope you can sort it out."

Having heard what she wanted, she relayed Aria's words to Edward. She added a bit of exaggeration, of course.

"She seems to resent you more than I had thought. She even wished you wouldn't return home when she lived with you."

"What? That ungrateful creature! I'm the one who raised her!"

As Edward expressed his uncontrollable anger, Iris watched with interest, then added, "And she said she once hoped you would just disappear."

"That terrible girl!" His face turned bright red.

Now the stage was set. It was time for the show to begin.

"There's nothing like conversation to handle matters like this, don't you think?" Iris said with a smile.

"It looks like you two have to talk about your feelings... I know of a party that Lady Aria will surely be attending soon."

"A party?" Edward said, his eyes gleaming. Ever since his decline in wealth, no one had invited him to one, and he had no clothes to wear to one either.

"You'll be able to get in if you come with me... and as you're going to speak with your daughter, I'll buy you some clothes to wear," Iris said, beaming.

It wasn't hard for her to guess what Edward would do at the party. He had no manners or shame, and if he was prodded in just the right way, he would throw a fit.

"Well, if you insist, I have no reason to refuse," Edward said, as though he were giving in for Iris' sake.

CHAPTER
ONE HUNDRED AND FOURTEEN

Edward had no intention of making up with his daughter in the first place. To him, his daughter was an inferior being, someone who existed to serve him and make his life better. Iris knew this, and she hadn't brought Edward to try to improve the relationship between them.

"I thought you had some unaired grudges against your father as well."

But she brazenly smiled at Aria, pretending she was acting purely out of goodwill.

Edward and Iris. It was a difficult sight to believe. It made no sense that Edward was here at all.

"Father."

"What's with that look on your face? You haven't seen your father in a long time, have you?" Edward looked at Aria with a frown. "Am I wrong to want to see my daughter?"

"No, not at all..."

"You know, I'm very upset with you, Aria. I'm still your father, you know."

When were you ever a proper father to her, you prick? I scowled at Edward in disbelief.

"Viscount Peridot, it's nice to meet you," I said, struggling to contain my anger. No matter what he said here, it was obvious it would not be good for Aria. My first priority was to get him out of here. "If you want to have a conversation with your daughter, I think a private place would be more suitable."

"I'd love to, but she refuses to come home," Edward said, scoffing.

I found this hilarious, because I knew how she'd been treated at home and what a scumbag he was, but the others present didn't know that. To them, Aria was a disrespectful lady who'd said she wished her father would disappear, staying at my mansion while refusing to speak to him.

The whispering slowly grew into a loud murmur that spread throughout the crowd. At this rate, it would only be a matter of time before the duchess heard of this. In fact, if the nasty-tempered Edward raised his voice a notch, he could get every single person here to stare at him.

In order to delay that disaster, I spoke up. "It doesn't have to be your home. I am acquainted with the people of this mansion, and I can ask for a private room where you two can speak.”

“I don’t understand why you’re so eager to send me away, but I have nothing to hide. Why shouldn’t I speak to her in public?” Edward shot back condescendingly.

“Look, Lady Mary is trying to hide something...”

“My goodness, a quiet lady like Lady Aria...”

People seemed to believe that Aria and I had something to hide.

“I’m not trying to hide anything. Go on and speak. If you’d like,” I said with gritted teeth.

Since the situation was unavoidable, I decided to hear the man out. *Why is he acting with such confidence?*

While I was quarreling with Edward, Aria was looking at someone else.

“Lady Iris...” she said, staring at Iris in shock.

Even I was bewildered, though I hadn’t spoken to Iris that many times. Of course, Aria was immensely troubled.

“Lady Aria, you said so yourself, didn’t you? Some people just don’t get along,” Iris said with a triumphant smile.

She was as hard to understand as Edward was. *What did Aria ever do to her? Why does she hate Aria so much? And why go to such lengths to be spiteful to another person?*

“Still, you should try to get along. You’re family, after all.”

Aria stared at Iris, unable to speak. I wanted to console her, but the situation didn't allow that.

"Hmm. You're probably wondering what the problem is, right?" Edward said, rubbing his chin and pretending to think. "As Lady Iris said, Aria and I are family. We must take care of each other whether we like it or not. But one of us has refused to talk and has shirked her duty. It left me deeply confused."

"Did you ever try to converse with her properly?" I scoffed. I didn't mean to sound this sarcastic, but that didn't matter.

"I wanted to, at times, but she ran off to your mansion. That's why a simple matter has become so complicated. Besides, Lady Mary, considering what you did..." Edward looked around arrogantly, shrugging and asking me if I was all right with him saying it. "In any case, I'll apologize if I've actually done anything wrong, Aria. You should come home now." He reached out his hand toward her, as if he were being generous. "You shouldn't be embarrassing yourself like this. Give it a little more time, and you'll see the error of your ways."

Perhaps encouraged by the eyes watching, Edward no longer hid his disdain for what Aria was doing.

I knew that Aria was tenderhearted, and the betrayal from Iris, whom she'd been close to recently, must be hurting like crazy. *I suppose it would be too much to ask her to respond to this properly.* I stepped forward to refute his words, taking a deep breath.

"I'm not embarrassed at all," came a firm voice from behind me before I could speak. "It was my decision, and I have nothing to be ashamed of."

"Did you just talk back to me?" Edward shouted, pointing his finger at his daughter angrily. It wasn't surprising that he was astonished; his daughter had never rebelled, no matter what he said, how much money he wasted, or how many drunken fits he threw.

Edward wasn't the only one taken aback; I also looked at her with wide eyes. Aria looked calm, contrary to my expectations, as she stared at her father.

"I'm not talking back to you. You're the one who asked for a conversation."

"How dare you..." Edward was about to raise his hand to slap her. Then he caught himself, looked around, and cleared his throat instead. Pretending to be a gentleman, he said, "Such a thing might be fun right now, but you'll only be happy if you marry a good man and start your own family."

Why aren't you mentioning the part where you latch yourself onto her parents-in-law like a leech?

"I decide what makes me happy, father. I am an adult. And besides—"

"What do you know?" Edward finally screamed, unable to rein in his temper.

The duchess and Ethen, who were standing some distance away, noticed what was going on and turned to look.

"My goodness, he's a barbarian!"

"No wonder we've never heard of him in high-society circles."

"Like father, like daughter, huh? He doesn't seem to feel any shame over causing a scene at the duchess' party."

People were saying rude things about Edward and Aria, but Edward continued to scream, oblivious to those around him.

"You seem to think you're talented, but that's not going to last long. Is it such a hard thing to ask that you marry someone and help out your father? Does your stupidity know no bounds?"

He had pretended to want civil conversation at first, but apparently his shallow patience had already run out. I wouldn't have minded if he made a fool of only himself like this, but the problem was that the more he screamed, the worse he made Aria look as well.

"Father. Calm down." Aria approached him, trying to soothe him, but Edward shouted louder.

"Perhaps it's because you never had a mother! You still can't think for yourself—"

"What is going on here?"

I knew this was going to happen. I bowed my aching head, one hand on my forehead. The duchess had walked over after noticing the commotion.

"I don't think you're on the guest list," she said with a frown.

Iris, who had been watching with an amused look on her face, came over with an innocent expression. "Your Grace, this is Viscount Peridot. He is Lady Aria's father."

"Viscount Peridot?"

"He said he wanted to speak with his daughter but felt hurt that he couldn't find the opportunity. I wanted to arrange a natural meeting, but... I think I've made a mistake."

Hurt, my ass! I wanted to scream at Iris to stop the disgusting act, but I was forced to bite my lip and hold back.

"What..." the duchess said.

This was the second time I'd inconvenienced the duchess. The first time might not have been my responsibility, but I'd made trouble again at a party the duchess had invited me to for the first time in years. I couldn't make a scene because I felt so ashamed.

"Lady Aria, what is going on here?" the duchess asked, as if to hear the story from the person directly involved.

"I—"

"No, you don't need to ask her. I will tell you," Edward said, cutting Aria off and stepping in between them. "She may be an adult, but she's my daughter, and yet unmarried. All I wanted to do was give her some advice as her father and ask her for some help." He thumped his chest as if deeply frustrated. "But here she is, showing such disrespect for her father. I couldn't help but lose my temper for a moment."

I looked at him in dismay as he acted as if he felt wronged.

Aria seemed to think it would be best to take Edward elsewhere instead of contradicting him, so she said politely, "Your Grace, I'm sorry we caused such a disturbance. Family matters are personal in nature, and I should have taken care of them in private. I feel bad that I've interrupted your party."

"Is he speaking the truth?" the duchess said with a frown.

"It's true that I left my father to live in the marquess' mansion."

"My goodness!"

The crowd began to murmur again, as if their suspicions had been confirmed.

Aria, what are you thinking? I bit my nails nervously, watching the situation unfold.

ONE HUNDRED AND FIFTEEN

"How could a child be so cold to her father, leaving him all alone while she chases her silly dream of becoming a singer?" Edward launched into a frantic rhetoric, seeing that Aria wasn't responding with any retorts. "I raised her! Any child should be of help to their parents. How could she leave me to fend for myself?"

What is the matter with him? I opened my mouth, determined to say something as he painted himself as the victim. "What are you—"

"I understand you feel upset with your daughter, but I'd rather you spoke of such things in a private place," the duchess interrupted with a displeased look on her face, glancing at Aria, then at Edward.

I remained where I stood, unable to approach the duchess or Aria. Frankly, I wanted to shout at Edward that he had been a poor excuse for a father, but I couldn't. This was the duchess' party. I felt guilty not only about the disturbances I'd caused the duchess—once by myself, and this time, by a guest I'd brought with me—but also because I planned to call off the engagement with her son. If this grew any worse, I would probably lose sleep at night from guilt toward Ethen and the duchess.

"I'm sorry, Your Grace, but…"

However, even then, Edward didn't have the manners to shut up. Apparently thinking he had an advantage, he said with a triumphant look on his face, "I am a member of the nobility! Am I supposed to do *labor* like commoners do? She leaves the house and lives in the lap of luxury, while I am left to take care of myself. What kind of daughter is she?" Edward dabbed his eyes, though there were no tears in them at all.

How could someone be so shameless?

"Do you find it embarrassing that you must work like the commoners to make money?" Aria, who had been listening quietly thus far, said slowly. I had no idea what she was planning.

"Of course I do! You talk about your fancy dreams of becoming a singer and are busy showing off in front of people in your expensive dresses. And yet you expect me to do what, do hard labor?" Edward said, clicking his tongue.

"I've never once been ashamed of working for money," Aria said, looking up. I was surprised to see confidence in her eyes. "I took up sewing and did it for money as soon as I was old enough to do so. I sometimes even played the piano, as my mother had taught me, for a small payment."

This set the guests murmuring again. She was speaking about something nobles would be embarrassed by, but she seemed to feel no humiliation at all.

"It was for my family and for you, father. I was working for my father, who had raised me. I never thought of it as shameful or too difficult."

"She sewed for money...?"

"Even so, she is a viscount's daughter. I pity her for having had to do such work for money since she was young."

A few people were whispering, directing sympathetic looks at Aria. Others were criticizing her, saying that it was only right to work and make money for her father.

"But still, wasn't it the viscount who reared her to the point where she could start making money on her own?"

"Her family has a title, and with enough money, she could have become a second wife for some rich family, at least. I think the effort is warranted, considering that her father holds the title..."

Unlike before, the opinions of the crowd were divided. It was progress, at least.

"Lady Aria, I know it can't have been easy for you, either," Iris said, breaking her silence and stepping forward. She seemed displeased that the situation wasn't going exactly as planned. "But the harder the situation gets, the more you should help your family. Think of how the viscount must have felt, having to ask you to work to feed him..."

"I think she's right. How it must have hurt his pride, having lived all his life as a noble!"

"Things must have been very difficult indeed."

A few credulous people nodded in agreement at Iris' words. *What a spineless bunch.* I felt a wave of disgust at the easily swayable crowd.

But Aria didn't seem at all fazed. "You may not be entirely happy with me because I didn't marry someone you wanted. But I've never done anything to feel guilty about."

"W-what?" Edward stammered, discomfited by Aria's firm response. He gritted his teeth and shouted angrily once more, "Is that right? What makes you so confident? You haven't done anything I asked!"

His reaction wasn't surprising. In the past, Aria would have been capable of nothing but apologizing no matter what absurdities he claimed.

"Did I really ask that much of you? I only asked that you marry into a good family. Don't I deserve to want that for my daughter?"

That wouldn't be a problem if it was really her happiness you wanted. But you just want to use her for your own gain. Why are you pretending to want what's best for her?

"Your happiness is mine, and vice versa. I guess you're too stupid to understand—"

"Enough," someone said, cutting him off. I looked up to see who'd said it.

It was the duchess, and she sounded angry.

I sighed. *Of course she's angry.* She had invited me, her son's fiancée, thinking I had finally started being reasonable. But this time, a lady I had brought caused a scene at the party. I would have hated the sight of me, too.

"Your Grace, I apologize for creating a disturbance at your party, but please do try to understand. You are a parent, too—"

"Why are you claiming that Lady Aria should marry someone she doesn't love to uphold your honor and support you, Viscount?" the duchess said.

Her words took everyone by surprise.

"I-I'm sorry?" Edward stammered.

I was stunned as well. I had assumed she would be upset about the disruption, but I never thought she would take a stance in this argument.

"I wasn't going to get involved in your family dispute, but if you're choosing to air your personal matters in public like this, I suppose what you really want is the public's opinion."

Edward, who had screamed at the top of his lungs in response to Aria's words, could only stutter after the duchess spoke. "Well… I… That's not what I…" He didn't seem to have the courage to talk back to the wife of the only duke in the empire and the host of this party. He was no longer capable of letting his anger show.

He looked around for someone to support him, and he found someone he could turn to.

"Ah, there you are. Lady Iris. Didn't you say you agreed with me?"

"What?" Iris said, looking deeply confused. She was as cornered as he was. Though she hadn't been the one to raise her voice, she had brought him here, claiming that she understood how he felt and taking upon herself the role of a mediator.

But I wasn't the only one who recognized this as a shallow excuse. Now that the duchess had openly countered Edward's argument, Iris was just as rattled as he was.

"I-I only brought you here so that you two could reach an understanding. I'm not in a position to offer my advice regarding a family matter," she said, trying not to get involved any further.

With no one to turn to, Edward pleaded with the duchess again. "She is my daughter, Your Grace! Her marriage would benefit not only me but also her even more."

"If you really wanted what was best for your daughter, you would give her a choice. From the look of things, you seem to be trying to say that Lady Aria has been staying at the marquess' mansion, trying to become a singer, and hasn't sent you any money to support you..." the duchess said, sounding as if she was repressing her anger. "It's not only children who have a duty to respect their parents. Parents must also treat their children fairly."

Edward quivered, speechless, and glowered at Aria, but that was all he could do. The moment the duchess took Aria's side, Edward's ability to persuade the crowd had vanished.

"The duchess is right."

"Yes. A child should treat their parents with respect, but this is too much."

A moment ago, it seemed that only half the crowd was on Aria's side. But a word from the duchess was enough to turn everyone against Edward.

"And I would like this argument to stop right here. As for you, Lady Aria..." the duchess said, basically asking Edward to leave.

Aria, who had looked confident thus far, turned nervously to the duchess. "I apologize for the disturbance, Your Grace."

"You don't need to apologize."

"Pardon?"

Aria, I, and everyone else who had been watching went wide-eyed, but the duchess said no more and turned away.

"What did she mean by saying Lady Aria doesn't have to apologize?"

"Perhaps she was being kind to the lady because she is Lady Mary's guest."

"Or perhaps she doesn't want Aria to feel sorry for Viscount Peridot?"

People were trying to guess what the duchess had meant, but the duchess walked into the mansion, saying she wanted to rest.

"No way..."

Someone was taking the opportunity to slip out of the crowd.

"Come with me." I had no intention of letting that woman escape. So, I told Aria quietly to follow me and set off after her.

CHAPTER ONE HUNDRED AND SIXTEEN

"Where are you going in such a hurry?" I called out to Iris when we were far enough away from the party for the murmuring of the crowd to fade away.

Iris stiffened and slowed to a stop, having apparently been unaware that she was being followed. "You must be gloating inside right now, since I've made a fool of myself," she said coldly, giving up on pretenses. "What an incredibly lucky girl you are. To be honest, it's enough to make me jealous. Would you care to share your secret? How do you paint yourself so successfully as someone so pitiful and worthy of protection?" she said to Aria, all her fake kindness gone from her face. It was clear she was being sarcastic.

Flabbergasted, I shot back, "Really? Paint herself as someone to be protected? Don't be absurd." *Is there no limit to her perversity? How could she say that?* "Do you think anyone who doesn't take your side is somehow deluded?"

"Of course I do. She has no background, and there is nothing going for her at all. But people are siding with her simply because you like her, Lady Mary," Iris said mockingly. She seemed to have given up on getting on my good side now that her plot had been exposed.

"You sound like Lady Aria stole your money or something."

"I hate her very much. Stole my money, you say? I'd much rather it was money." Clenching her fists, she glared at Aria. There had been no quarrel between them. I wondered what Iris was claiming Aria had taken from her.

"The mere fact that she's taken up a spot next to you, Lady Mary, irks me so much. She is the daughter of a mere viscount, and one in nothing but name. Who does she think she is?" she muttered angrily.

That's the only reason? Why is she making such a big deal out of it and of Aria's lack of status?

I slowly opened my mouth to argue with her, but Aria was faster.

"What do *you* think I am? Is there a reason I can't be friends with Mary?"

"Ha! Are you seriously asking me that question?" Iris said with a laugh. "There is such a thing as rank within our society. I don't know what sugarcoated words you used to attach yourself to people like some parasite, but do you think doing that will boost your own status?"

"What are you…" Aria frowned, as if she found this hard to understand.

But Iris continued to spout nonsense. This was not so much a conversation as a monologue.

"Look at Lady Ashley or Lady Maia, for instance. They know their place. They know exactly what kind of person deserves to be Lady Mary's friend, so they never act like they are her friends."

It was true that I couldn't really call them my friends; my parents had only introduced me to them, children of their clients, to teach me how to socialize. The two had never acted overly familiar, while I talked to them like they were beneath me. That was enough to show that we were not on equal footing with each other.

"You're not at their social level. You're basically a commoner. Shouldn't that tell you something? It annoys me no end that you flaunt your supposed friendship with her, like you really are her friend."

"Flaunt my friendship? I never—"

"It's just like your father said. You seem to think you've become someone special after singing a few times in the street. Let me tell you this clearly. You are a nobody. You wouldn't even be able to feed yourself without Lady Mary's help. So, what gives you the confidence?" Iris spat venomously, as if releasing all the hatred she had built up inside herself.

I had no idea why she'd made such a big deal of social status, propriety, and whatnot. I wanted Aria to handle this matter on her own, but I could no longer bear to simply watch.

Taking a step closer to Iris, I said, "She needs to know her place, huh? Now that is very interesting."

I knew that this society was strictly status-based—people had incessantly talked about praise from commoners being worthless. But just because that was how society here was structured, it did not mean that I had to think about status when I picked my friends.

"I'd like to say the same to you. Do you have any right to meddle in who I choose to be friends with?"

"You might say I have none, since I am not your family or your friend. But I'm merely saying something that any other lady would agree with." Iris flinched but held her head high. "You are not an ordinary person, Lady Mary. One might argue that you stand right in the center of high society as a whole. Of course you should choose friends—"

"So, do you mean to suggest that you're suitable and Aria is not?" I said, frustrated.

Iris bit her lip as if her pride was hurt. "It doesn't have to be me... but you should at least choose someone from a family that won't embarrass you—"

"Embarrass me? In front of whom? I don't feel embarrassed at all. I don't have to let the opinions of others sway what I do. Nobody has the right to meddle in my life."

I couldn't understand Iris at all. We were basically strangers, and it was none of her business how I chose to live my life or whom I spent time with. *So why is she so obsessed with my behavior and my friendships, acting like it is insulting to see me with Aria?*

"It's none of your concern how I live my life. What are you, jealous?" I said with a click of the tongue. I wasn't sure if "jealousy" was the right word, but her actions were difficult to understand.

Iris quivered as she balled her fists. "Jealous? Please don't be absurd."

"Then why in the world would you—"

"I did my best."

Did what? I thought, staring at her in confusion. She looked ready to cry at any moment.

"I did my best to be worthy of your friendship. No matter how much people mocked me or laughed at me, I never gave up."

Come to think of it, I remembered hearing that she had followed me around for a while, along with Ashley and Maia. I recalled my first meeting with her. She had seemed angry that I'd poured a drink on her dress on purpose and humiliated her in public.

"I wouldn't have minded as much if a suitable person had taken that place next to you. What is the reason you can't accept me but can accept Lady Aria? You said you were embarrassed to have me around."

From what Iris was saying, however, the matter did not seem all that simple.

"You should have picked someone worthy of you, at least. Did you humiliate me like that just so you could spend time with a nobody like her?"

So, this was all the result of the real Mary's rude behavior. Feeling a bit apologetic, I went silent.

"I wouldn't be so upset if you'd kept on ignoring everybody, like you always did. But you had to pick this girl off the street and make me feel—" Unable to finish her sentence, Iris looked angrily Aria.

Though I couldn't understand it completely, I thought I could tell where her anger had come from. Not that this justified her behavior.

"Then why didn't you come to me with this question from the start?"

If she'd been upset because she'd been ignored, and miserable because Aria had become my friend and she didn't... then her anger should have been directed at me.

"You weren't brave enough to do that, so you chose someone easier to pick on and caused this mess. You didn't even manage to speak to her openly, going behind her back and bringing her father into this."

The way she'd chosen to vent her sense of inferiority and hatred had been the worst approach possible.

"You call her a nobody, but I don't understand why you fail to recognize your own pettiness," I spat angrily.

She bit her lip, unable to respond. I wasn't sure if she was out of things to say or if she considered it not to be "her place," as she'd been droning on about.

"Are you done talking?" I asked.

She said nothing.

"Then apologize," I said, glancing at Aria. Whatever the case, Aria was the victim in all this. And for a brief period, Aria had considered Iris a friend, telling her details about her life that could be used against her. An apology would not be enough to mend things, but I stepped back, deciding it was up to them to wrap up the matter.

"I..." Aria said with difficulty, after watching our conversation without being able to say a single word. "I didn't know you were thinking such things. I understand now why you behaved the way you did... but that doesn't mean I have to forgive you."

Iris glared at Aria, and Aria continued calmly, "It was by coincidence that Mary and I became friends. Just because you hate seeing me sing doesn't mean I have to give up on my dream."

"Ha..." Iris gave a sigh that was equal parts sarcastic and mocking.

"So that's why—"

"That's enough. I don't want to hear you brag any longer. I have nothing more to say to you."

She's still so arrogant! I tried to grab her as she cut Aria off and went to leave, but her next words stopped me and Aria in our tracks.

"And Lady Mary, you asked why I wasn't able to talk to you about it in person earlier." She stared at Aria with a smirk on her face. "Isn't that funny? Lady Aria wouldn't have been able to say a word to me either if you hadn't been so supportive."

With that, Iris turned around and walked away.

CHAPTER
ONE HUNDRED AND SEVENTEEN

Maybe I should have left Aria and Iris to talk it out among themselves, but I couldn't hold myself back.

After a brief silence, I spoke up carefully. "You don't have to listen to her. It doesn't matter who says it, as long as it's the right thing to say. She just refuses to admit she's wrong, doesn't she?" I said, glancing at Aria cautiously.

"I'm fine," she said, after staring down the corridor where Iris had gone. "Perhaps she's not entirely wrong."

"Don't pay that any mind. There's no logic to her words, and she's just trying to be spiteful." I was angry that Iris had said such a thing to Aria, who was already lacking in self-confidence.

"I wish I could still be confident after hearing such words."

"As I said, there's no need to listen—"

"Lady Mary," came a voice from behind.

Oh, right. I nearly forgot about him.

"Are you all right?"

It seemed Ethen had been looking for me, having seen the duchess off. No doubt he was confused since both the host and the main guest had disappeared.

"You must have been shocked—"

"I'm fine," I said, cutting him off as I turned away. "You should be more concerned about your mother. And you should stay at the party as a member of the hostess' family—"

"That's all right. I can go back with you now."

He knew that I would never become a part of this family. *Why is he burdening me like this?* I couldn't reveal my emotions in front of Aria, so I chose to keep my mouth shut.

"Your father has left the mansion," Ethen said to Aria, after gazing at me for a while as I refused to say anything further. "Since my mother spoke that way earlier, nobody will be rude to you if you go back to the party."

"I see. Thank you for telling me," Aria said with a forced smile.

I didn't want her to go back to the party. Although Edward had left and there was no one who would be openly rude to her, there was no way she would want to go back to that battlefield. People might not say anything, but it was obvious they would stare at her as if she was some sort of spectacle.

"I think we should call it a day," I said. I thought that it would be best for us to leave, but Aria, not Ethen, stopped me.

"No, that won't be necessary," she said. "Mary, you don't have to go home. Lord Ethen is here…"

"Are you saying you'll go back on your own?" I asked, surprised.

Aria nodded. "I'm really fine. But if I went inside with you, people would stare at you, too, and possibly inconvenience you."

I preferred that over letting her leave alone or spending time at the party with Ethen. "You're in no position to be worried about me," I said.

"This is my personal business. I don't want to let it affect you, Mary," she said firmly.

I stopped protesting, unable to say anything further. If it burdened her more for me to try and stop her, then perhaps it would be better to talk things over with her later and let her go home for now.

"I'm really fine. Don't worry. See you later." Aria nodded to Ethen briefly and strode away. Though she said she was fine, I knew she would continue to mull over Iris' words. Unable to stop her or chase after her, I stared at her as she walked away.

"How is the duchess doing?" I asked Ethen quietly, breaking the awkward silence that had ensued between us.

He sounded dismissive, as if there was no reason for concern. "My mother is fine. She's not angry at Lady Aria either, so you needn't worry."

"After all this?" I couldn't believe his words and looked up at him. Something like this happened immediately after I'd been invited by her again. Perhaps she was frustrated inside, even if she wasn't showing it. "I couldn't have made too good an impression on her the last time I met her. What terrible luck I have—"

"Lady Mary, there is no need for you to think that," he said, cutting me off. "My mother isn't angry because of you. Please don't think that."

"She might think that this happened because of a guest I brought."

"It wasn't Lady Aria's fault, and it most definitely wasn't yours," he said firmly, trying to soothe me. "If you're concerned about sending Lady Aria away on her own, I can send someone to bring her back."

"There's no need." Our relationship was already awkward enough, and I didn't want to ruin it any further, so I just shook my head.

Even though I hate the idea, I should still go back to the party. Aria had probably gone home, and I could see her afterward. It would not be too late for a conversation then.

"Let's go back in," I said, getting a hold of myself with an effort and walking ahead.

"Weren't you shocked?" Ethen asked worriedly.

Shocked? Of course I was. I knew that Iris had never really liked Aria, but she had approached Aria first to apologize and defended her in public, so I thought that she had changed. Because I was also living with the burden of my past actions, I had not thought to doubt her. I believed that people could change.

But she hadn't changed at all. In fact, she'd been growing her hatred in the dark.

"Lady Iris must be out of her mind," I said rather bluntly.

I lapsed into thought. Iris had gone too far. Her malice had been too intense for this to have been a way to simply humiliate Aria. During her conversations with Aria, she must have realized what sort of person Edward was. And a few minutes with him would have been enough to tell her what scum she was dealing with.

Despite that, she'd made all of this happen. That meant she didn't care how much Aria would be hurt or the way she would be branded in the public eye. And the only reason was that Aria did not deserve her current position. It was hard to understand.

"What is the big deal with her and her obsession with ranks? I suppose being my friend is something to be proud of, but not being my friend is not the end of the world." Looking back on the incident only made me angrier. Forgetting that I'd been avoiding Ethen all this time, I muttered, "Even if Aria and I weren't friends, that doesn't mean that she would get to be in Aria's place. And if she felt hurt by the incident between us, she should have spoken to me."

I was thinking out loud. Ethen listened quietly to my annoyed words and slowed down to match his pace with mine.

"Why would she do such a thing? I don't think I will ever understand Lady Iris."

"She probably thinks something that should have been hers was taken away from her," he said mildly.

"It was never hers to begin with!"

"I don't think Lady Iris' actions can be justified in any way, but I do think I understand why she did it."

My ears pricked up as I came to a stop. "Why do you think she did it?" I asked, turning around. Her actions were far too atrocious to be motivated by a mere sense of inferiority. Knowing the reason wouldn't help me understand her any better, but I was still curious as to what Ethen thought it was.

"She feels inferior to someone who easily took the spot she's so desired all along," he said, stopping too. "Everyone knew that Lady Iris wanted to be close to you."

Was it that obvious? I didn't really know anything about this, so I let him continue.

"Count Mirvaseba is also someone who fixates on his friendships. No doubt there was some of his influence on her way of thinking. Her goal was probably to become your friend, and her failure to do so might have caused her family to pressure her."

This stupid status-based society. Frustrated, I shook my head.

"But that friendship she wanted so badly was given to Lady Aria, even though she was not actively trying to attain it."

Ethen's sensible explanation helped me finally see where Iris' rage had come from. Had she felt upset because Aria had taken something she wanted and seemed to take it for granted?

"Not that I think her way of expressing her frustration was right. But I can understand how she might have felt," he said with a smile that showed his complicated feelings.

Does this mean Ethen has felt something similar before? "Did you ever feel that way, Lord Ethen?" I found myself asking.

When I realized what I'd done and covered my mouth, it was too late. It could have been a sensitive question, and I'd asked it without thinking. *What the hell am I doing?* There was no way to take back the words now.

"Not as deeply as Lady Iris, but I think I know what it feels like," he said, blinking slowly.

Not wanting to ask any further, I quickly changed the subject. We'd been talking about unpleasant things all day, and I had the feeling that the mood would become unbearably uncomfortable if we talked any more about this.

"I'm worried about whether we can keep the mood of the party cheerful until the duchess returns. I mean, after what just happened..." I said, turning my head away.

Ethen looked at me with an unreadable expression on his face. Perhaps I had reminded him of something unpleasant after all. Feeling guilty, I looked at him apologetically.

"You don't have to tell me what it was. I have no intention of prying—"

"I'm more than willing to explain if you're the one asking," he said cryptically, meeting my eyes. "That means there is something you still want to know about me, does it not?"

Ethen had always been excessively careful and chivalrous around me, but here he was, suddenly being so bold. I was so astounded that I could do nothing but blink.

CHAPTER ONE HUNDRED AND EIGHTEEN

"Why would she do such a thing? I don't think I will ever understand Lady Iris."

When Mary said that, Ethen recalled Iris' actions. He thought he could understand why she had done what she had done. He had also felt a similar emotion before.

"She probably thinks something that should have been hers was taken away from her."

"It was never hers to begin with!" Mary muttered under her breath.

Ethen pondered her words for a moment, then said, "I don't think Lady Iris' actions were justifiable, but I do think I understand why she did it."

He could see himself in Iris. Though he was nowhere near as malicious as she was, he was like her in terms of wanting something so desperately.

"Why do you think she did it?" Mary looked at him with widened eyes. She was asking because she really didn't understand, but Ethen did not respond, gazing into her red eyes instead.

Oh... how long has it been since I've seen those eyes empty of any anxiety or apology?

Ethen knew that this was only a temporary change, but he was glad to see it. The fact that she would ask him something with no reserve was enough to make him happy.

A moment later, as he stared down at her, he slowly said, "She feels inferior to someone who easily took the spot she's so desired all along." He summarized Iris' actions in one sentence.

"Count Mirvaseba is also someone who fixates on his friendships. No doubt there was some of his influence on her way of thinking. Her goal was probably to become your friend, and her failure to do so might have caused her family to pressure her."

Count Mirvaseba was famous for his greed, and the things he was most obsessed with were connections and information. His daughter, Iris, and his son and Iris' older brother, Rubin, were both respected in high society, but it wasn't likely that they had willingly worked for that social standing. Even if they did not aspire to be at the top of high society, if they wanted to go anywhere near it, they needed the friendship of Mary, the marquess' daughter. Mary, however, did not let anyone in that easily.

"But that friendship she wanted so badly was given to Lady Aria, even though she was not actively trying to attain it."

Mary looked down at the floor, seemingly deep in thought.

Oops. I hope she doesn't think I'm taking Lady Iris' side. Wanting to hide the fact that he felt the tiniest bit of sympathy for Iris, Ethen quickly added, "Not that I think her way of expressing her frustration was right. But I can understand how she might have felt."

"Did you ever feel that way, Lord Ethen?" Mary asked, raising her head slowly and looking at him.

He was caught off guard, not having expected this question. If it had been from anyone else, he would have taken the question to be rude, but he didn't hate that she was asking something about him.

"Not as deeply as Lady Iris, but I think I know what it feels like," he said.

At least, it meant she was curious about him.

He waited for her to ask another question, but she turned away with an awkward look on her face.

"I'm worried about keeping the mood of the party cheerful until the duchess returns. I mean, after what just happened..."

Although she had been angry at Lady Iris' rude behavior, at least she hadn't seemed to feel awkward while in conversation with him. But now she was back to being uncomfortable, and Ethen did his best to hide his hurt.

This was their first meeting since she'd asked to call off their engagement. He had sent her letter after letter, but never once did she respond to any of them. It was clear that she was here today to hide the fact that they'd decided to break the engagement off and had chosen to stay because she felt apologetic toward the duchess. If he let her go now, he would likely never see her again before the month was over.

He grew nervous at the thought, avoiding her gaze and clenching his fists.

"You don't have to tell me what it was. I have no intention of prying—" she said.

"I'm more than willing to explain if you're the one asking," he replied. It had been completely on impulse. She would never give him another opportunity after today. He would regret letting her leave for the rest of his life if he didn't try something. It would be preferable to try to stop her from leaving, even if it made him seem impetuous.

"That means there is something you still want to know about me, does it not?"

It didn't matter if this confused her. He didn't care if she thought he was strange. "I'd rather you asked." He gazed at Mary, who was wide-eyed and blinking.

He could see the astonishment in her expression, but he didn't mind. If he could avoid regret, he could live with a little embarrassment. That would be better than never being allowed to see her again and living with regret all his life.

He would act as out of character as necessary to stop her from leaving.

I blinked, unable to hide my confusion at his words. *Has he always been this assertive? I don't think so.* As a matter of fact, he liked to err on the side of caution.

"Is it too much to ask?" Ethen asked, sounding downcast.

Pulling myself together, I asked slowly, "Would you mind if I asked you... why you felt that way?" I had to admit I was curious, just a little. Ethen and jealousy didn't really seem to go hand in hand. *What made this gentle person feel envious?*

"It wasn't exactly like what Lady Iris felt. It was something far more trivial, to the point of being embarrassing..." Ethen blushed when I asked him as he'd wanted. In fact, he looked sort of cute as he fumbled for his words, which was definitely not normal for him.

Wait, cute? That won't do. Pull yourself together. We're going to be strangers when the month is over.

Clearing my throat in an attempt to push the thought away, I said, "Of course you shouldn't feel the way Lady Iris felt."

"In hindsight, I do feel a little ashamed of myself..." The redness spread across his face and to the tips of his ears. "The first name..."

He said no more after that. *The first name? This has to do with a name? What is he saying?* I looked at him, puzzled, but he seemed unable to continue. I tilted my head in confusion as he held himself back so much that I was slightly annoyed.

"I envied the way Lady Aria used... the first name."

Who is he talking about? I stared up at him stupidly, then belatedly realized what he meant.

"Wait, are you referring to my name?"

His silence was all the answer I needed. *No way. This is absurd!*

As if it wasn't surprising enough that Ethen had been jealous of anyone, it was Aria that he'd envied, and it was because we called each other by our first names.

I recalled the time he had tried to say something but cut himself short just as we'd started doing that. *Has this been on his mind ever since?*

"B-but that's nothing..." I didn't have to look in the mirror to know that my face was extremely red. *You seriously felt jealous over that?* That was what I wanted to ask, but I thought it would seem silly to do so when I was blushing so hard.

"Actually... it was the wish I wanted to ask of you..." he said quietly, staring at the floor.

The wish? Is he referring to the wish I'd promised him if he won the hunting competition?

The only reason he had tried so hard to win was simply because he wanted us to be on a first-name basis.

I stared at his face, speechless. No one had ever been so affectionate toward me before.

"You shouldn't use your wish on something like that. That would be a waste," I grumbled, unable to stand the awkwardness.

But Ethen sounded firm, though his face was even redder than mine. "It is not a waste at all."

I couldn't reply.

"How can it be a waste to use a wish for something that's going to improve our relationship?"

I knew I shouldn't be interested in him, but when he acted this way, I kept considering other possibilities. I wished I wasn't Mary Bell.

If only Aria and Edville had become a couple, as they should have, I would not be feeling so guilty. The confidence in Ethen's eyes and in his feelings made me want to take his hand, no matter how much I told myself that it wasn't the right thing to do.

I stared into his eyes for a while. "Why... do you like me?" I asked as if possessed by something.

Why does he like me at all? I had a filthy tongue, and all I had ever done was inconvenience him. Even after I had entered Mary's body, I hadn't done anything to be of help to him. If anything, I'd requested excessive favors and subtly tried to put Aria and him together. The most I'd done was try to avoid him, and I never tried to make a good impression on him.

I wondered what I would have liked about me if I was in his shoes. I came up completely empty. It would have been easier to understand if he hated me.

Why does he like me? What did I ever do to make myself worthy of such affection? I couldn't understand him in the least.

Ethen blinked, surprised, then smiled faintly. "Why, you ask?" Ethen looked at me with the straightforward eyes that I dearly liked and therefore wanted to avoid. He took a deep breath as if he had a lot of things to say, then opened his mouth.

CHAPTER
ONE HUNDRED AND NINETEEN

"I like seeing you being passionate about something."

I blinked at his vague answer, but Ethen continued in a calm voice.

"If you could see how your eyes glitter when you see something you like and realize how attractive you are at that moment, I'm sure you'd understand how I feel," he said, his eyes glowing. "I find your confidence charming and the willpower to carry out your plans lovely."

Lovely? Nobody had ever called me that before. I stood still, unable to respond.

"Hmm, I have so many things to say that I'm not sure where to start."

"Of course you do..." *Why did I say that?* My mouth was spewing nonsense as usual.

"Of course, many people like you and wish to be friends with you," he said, laughing. "That means I will have to put in the effort if I'm to become your priority. I'm not ready to give up just because you're not willing to reciprocate my feelings at this moment."

How can I refuse him in a way that hurts him as little as possible? I thought. But as always, my efforts to think turned out to be useless. My lips moved as if they had a will of their own, completely ignoring how I actually felt.

"Please don't like me. It's tiresome."

Tiresome was certainly not the correct word to describe my feelings. They were something deeper and more difficult to describe, but suddenly they were labeled as simply "tiresome." It was a careless, even infuriating, response, but Ethen didn't seem to mind.

"But I still don't want to give up. That's how feelings work." Ethen tucked my hair, which was fluttering in the wind, behind my ear. "I'll do my best to win you over. I swear."

"My lord, there you are," said an old butler, approaching us from a distance. "I think you should head back to the party."

"I was just about to," Ethen replied. He moved his hand, which had been cautiously caressing my hair, away. "May I escort you?" He held out his hand.

We had to return to the garden, where the party was still in full swing. That meant we had to play the part of a loving couple. I silently took his hand. Mine was trembling, but neither of us acknowledged it.

It wasn't because I hated taking his hand, but because I was afraid. I was afraid that feelings I'd rather not be aware of would somehow carry over to him. They were emotions I had no business having, and I didn't want them to grow.

"Please don't worry about Lady Iris. I knew she would cause a scene at some point." Lady Zir, who'd openly displayed her hostility toward me and Aria at the hunting competition, sidled up to me and consoled me as if we were lifelong friends. "My goodness, it was obvious the man was out of his mind! To think she brought such a man to the duchess' party..."

I had no patience left to listen to her. "I'm not worried."

"Pardon?" Lady Zir said, her eyes wide.

"So please don't bother," I said, showing my displeasure.

I'd been hanging around at the party to allow Ethen and the duchess to save face, but I could no longer stand this. My thoughts were in terrible disarray.

"Lady Mary, where are you going?"

Ashley and Maia followed me with worried looks on their faces.

"I'm leaving. My head hurts. I can't bear to sit at this party anymore."

"Well... that's not surprising."

"Lady Aria must have been shocked, too. Please tell her things will be fine."

The two of them didn't try to stop me from leaving. I guess *I should go and offer an excuse to Ethen and the duchess, too.* I went to Ethen first.

"I have a bit of a headache. I'm sorry, but I think I'll have to leave. Can I say goodbye to the duchess?"

"Are you all right?" he asked, looking concerned.

"It's nothing serious. I think some rest is all I need."

"I'll see you off—"

"You should not leave this party twice in a row. The guests would be alarmed," I said.

Ethen seemed to agree that leaving again in the duchess' absence would be too much. He sighed quietly. "Let me take you to my mother, then."

I couldn't bring myself to refuse this last bit of goodwill from him, so I followed him into the mansion.

"So, you're leaving?"

"Yes, Your Grace. My companion has already left, and I have a headache."

Thankfully, the duchess did not seem all that angry. She studied me with a look of concern.

"Dear me. Please go home and rest. I'll be in touch."

"Are you feeling well, Your Grace?" I asked.

Her eyes widened for a moment, then she smiled. "I'd be lying if I said I wasn't surprised, but it wasn't your fault. Please don't pay it any mind and go get some rest. Ethen? See her off, please."

"No, he should remain at the party—"

"Actually, I was just about to go back. Haha. I can't get in between you two when things are going so well, can I?" she said, covering her mouth with a fan and laughing. She was probably trying to be considerate in her own way, but it really wasn't necessary.

Not that I could refuse her, of course.

I forced a smile. "I'll be taking my leave. I hope to see you again, Your Grace."

The opposite is what I really want. I left the mansion with Ethen.

"I'll be in touch," he said.

"I can't tell you for certain that I'll be able to respond," I said, turning away from him. There was still a pile of his unopened letters on my desk. I wasn't brave enough to read them, much less write a reply. My voice was cold, but Ethen didn't seem to mind.

"Still, you might feel the urge to read my letters one day and even respond to them."

I didn't reply.

"I can't miss my chance by failing to write on that particular day, right?"

Why does this man behave as if he has no pride when it comes to me?

I had no idea if he knew how complicated my thoughts had become as he walked me to the carriage. He held my hand and helped me into the carriage, and I tried to keep my eyes averted.

"Thank you. Goodbye."

"Have a safe trip back," he said, kissing the back of my hand briefly and letting go. I wasn't looking at him, so I couldn't tell what kind of expression was on his face. But I could certainly guess.

The door closed softly.

I decided to meet with Aria first and tell her that she didn't have to worry about what had happened today. Thankfully, the duchess had rebuked Iris and Edward, which meant that Aria's reputation wouldn't suffer much damage.

Things will be fine.

While I considered various things with a hand on my aching head, I arrived at the mansion.

What awaited me wasn't Aria, but the beginning of yet another incident.

"She isn't back yet?"

Aria had left the party at least an hour before I had, but she was not at the mansion. I grabbed Annie and asked her where Aria was, but the girl looked more shocked than I was.

"I-I assumed she would come back with you, my lady."

She really seemed to have no idea, so I went to find the horseman instead. I had assumed she'd taken a carriage back to the mansion. *Where did she go?*

"My lady?"

"Where is Aria?"

"Pardon?" The horseman seemed extremely confused. "She came back here, didn't she?"

"I'm asking because she isn't here. Did you drop her off here?" I demanded.

The man turned pale. Something seemed to be bothering him. "S-she hasn't come to the mansion?"

Getting an ominous feeling, I asked, "Tell me everything that happened while you were giving her a ride, from beginning to end."

"W-well... Lady Aria came out and told me that she would be returning early. I wanted to come back to the mansion, of course. But..."

"But?" I stared at him viciously.

He fell flat on his face out of fear. "Please, forgive me!" he begged.

"Who told you to kneel? I told you to tell me what happened!" I said, startled by his action. I reached for him, intending to pull him up, but he screamed and backed away, perhaps thinking I would hit him or something.

"Oh goodness me!"

"Mr. Hans. What are you doing?" Lilian said, coming out of nowhere. She helped the man up, and I was finally able to hear a proper account.

"Y-you see... I was going to bring her here, of course, but she asked me to drop her off on our way back, saying she had to visit somewhere."

"She did? Where was this?"

"Well... it was close to the entrance of the downtown area."

I remembered Ashley saying she'd seen Aria downtown as well. *Does this have something to do with that?*

"And you just let her go?"

"She told me she had enough money to get herself a carriage home and said I should come back here... I'm sorry, my lady. She said she would be back soon..." the horseman said, bowing repeatedly.

I ignored the man and turned to Lilian. "Send some people downtown to look for her."

"Yes, my lady."

Aria was no child, and she might simply have wanted to get some air, but it was worrisome that she had vanished after what had happened today.

Moments later, a few servants from the mansion left for the downtown area at Lilian's request. But this did not make me feel much better.

"I hope she's all right..."

I chewed my fingernails as I waited for news. I had come home to rest, but I didn't get any of that. Instead, I paced around the garden for a long time.

"That's a carriage..."

As the sun was about to set, a carriage pulled up to the mansion. I ran toward it with no thought of my dignity or pride.

CHAPTER ONE HUNDRED AND TWENTY

"Oh..."

When I went outside to the carriage, I realized it wasn't who I'd been waiting for.

"Why did you leave without telling me? And why didn't you send the carriage back?"

It was May in the carriage, not Aria. I'd been all over the place throughout the day, so I had forgotten about him altogether. Because the horseman had panicked and failed to return to the duke's mansion, May had been forced to call a private carriage to get home.

"How is Lady Aria?"

"It's none of your business," I said, turning away with a disappointed look.

"Hey, that's not fair," May said, shaking his head weakly as if he had no energy left to be angry at me anymore.

"My lady... Oh, you're back, my lord," Lilian said as she approached, noticing May, and greeting him. May gave up on getting news of Aria from me and turned to Lilian.

"Where is Lady Aria?"

"Oh, Lady Aria is…" Lilian glanced over at me, then came toward me and said, "My apologies. I sent knights to look for her, but they couldn't find her."

"What are you talking about?" May asked. "Are you saying Lady Aria is missing?"

"That's right. She said she would come back here, but she got out of the carriage somewhere else. And she hasn't returned."

May's head shot up as he realized the gravity of the situation. His eyes pointed toward the sky. Noticing that the sun was setting, a grim frown appeared on his face.

"The sun is about to set. She still hasn't come back?"

"No. And we sent people to look for her where the horseman let her off, but they couldn't find her. Today's incident must have been so much for her to handle. Why did she have to disappear like this, too?" I said, chewing my fingernails.

May pulled my hand away from my mouth. "You didn't even get a message? She wouldn't vanish like this without telling you."

"You think I would be this worried if there had been a message?" I spat irritably.

May tutted quietly. He seemed worried about Aria as well. He called the horseman back even though he'd just gotten off the carriage.

"Where did you let her off?" he asked.

"N-near the downtown entrance, my lord."

"You didn't see where she was headed?"

The horseman struggled to remember, but then he seemed to hit upon something and clapped. "Oh! I remember it being near a dressmaker's shop. I offered to take her to her destination since it seemed unkind to simply drop her off at the entrance. And she told me to drop her off near the dressmaker's shop instead."

A dressmaker's shop? It was the last place I expected Aria to go, but she could have gone someplace nearby, not necessarily the shop.

"Shall we send people there again?" Lilian asked.

The sun had nearly set, and I was worried because we still had not heard anything from Aria.

"Yes. I'll go as well."

After pacing near the door for a while, we pulled ourselves together and stepped outside the mansion. That was when a dull looking boy stopped us.

"E-excuse me."

"What do you want?" I asked.

The boy trembled, apparently terrified by my simple question. *Do I look that scary?* I fell silent, unnerved by the boy's response, and May spoke to the boy instead.

"What is it?"

"Uh, I was told to bring this letter to this mansion as quickly as possible."

A letter? Maybe it's Ethen. It can't be that urgent. I ignored it. "We don't have time to be reading letters—"

"Just a moment," May said, noticing something and taking the letter. "It's from Lady Aria."

May had discovered her name written on the envelope. I snatched it from him when I realized this.

"Where did you get this, and from whom?" May asked.

The child thought about it carefully. "Downtown... I was selling flowers with my brother. A lady with blonde hair asked me to do an errand and said that she would pay me."

"Do you remember what she looked like?"

"Uh... she had green eyes. She was pretty like an angel."

It was clear that Aria had handed the letter to the boy. Getting impatient, I put a hand on his shoulder. "Did she have anyone with her? How did she look?"

"Calm down. You're going to make him cry," May said, pushing me back.

"Did you come here as soon as you got the letter?"

"Yes."

"On foot?"

The mansion was at least thirty minutes by foot from the downtown area. This was a child, so it must have taken at least an hour.

"Yes."

"Was the lady alone?"

"Yes, she was. But she said she was in a hurry because someone was waiting for her. She left right after she gave me the letter."

The child didn't seem scared of May at all. That left me feeling odd, but it couldn't be helped. I crossed my arms and watched as May soothed the boy and got more information from him.

"All right. Thank you for delivering the letter. Here's a tip for your trouble."

"Huh? The lady already paid me."

"Think of it as a bonus. Hans? Take this boy back downtown," May said, handing a few coins to the boy. "It doesn't seem like anything happened to her. Read the letter first."

I opened the letter and read the contents. This was the first letter she'd ever written me. Written in neat handwriting was the following:

I am sorry I left without telling you, Mary. I am sure you must be worried about what happened today. I assure you that I am all right. However, I do feel bad for possibly inconveniencing you.

I would like to stay elsewhere for a few days. It is not only because of today's incident. I do not want to be a burden to you, Mary. I am not going back to my father's house, so please do not worry too much.

Lady Priscilla will be giving a performance three days from now. Let us watch it and go home together in better spirits. It would be even better if you came with Lord Ethen.

See you then.

—Aria

Inside the letter were two tickets to the concert.

I let out a sigh, feeling a mixture of relief and fatigue as I placed my hand on my forehead. She'd sent a letter, which meant things couldn't be that bad. But that didn't mean I was happy with the situation.

"What does it say?"

"She says she needs a few days to clear her head."

Putting the letter and tickets back inside the envelope, I started to trudge along. My head hurt, but since she'd said she was fine, I decided to go home and rest for the time being.

"It's only been a day, but I feel so tired," I muttered, walking back toward the mansion.

The three days passed quickly, though I had no idea how they'd gone by. I spent at least a day and a half staring into space. Aria had been my only hobby, burden, and mission. With her gone, I almost felt empty inside.

"Mary, are you sure you're all right?"

My mother, my father, and even May seemed worried upon seeing me do nothing all day but stare out the window.

"It's nice that you're so close to Lady Aria, but her life isn't yours. What's the need to be so upset?" May finally said, reaching the end of his rope.

But I merely told him, "It's none of your business."

You can only say that because you don't know how the plot of this novel goes.

If it hadn't been for me, Aria would have been guaranteed a happy, peaceful ending. Well, perhaps not entirely peaceful, but the struggles would have been temporary. My presence in this world kept causing incidents that were not supposed to happen, and I had the feeling she was being pushed farther and farther away from her happy ending. *How can I not be upset?*

Aria had sent me two tickets so that I could take Ethen along, but I hadn't even read his letters yet. I didn't particularly relish the fact that more of them were piling up on my desk by the day.

"Jeez, you have your fiancé. Why give this to me?" May complained.

In the end, I gave the extra ticket to May. I couldn't let the ticket go to waste since Aria had bought it, so this was the best thing I could think of.

"I'm giving it to you for a reason. Must I explain myself to you every single time?" I said irritably.

"You know what? Whatever. I've been worried about Lady Aria anyway," he said, scratching his neck.

I couldn't believe that we were meeting at a concert after spending three days apart, though it was just like something Aria would do.

Taking a deep breath, I left the mansion.

"As expected of one of Lady Priscilla's performances. Look at all these people."

Though it wasn't as crowded as her comeback performance, where I'd seen her for the first time, the hall was still full of people.

"Lady Priscilla is releasing a new song today."

"I'm so excited! What kind of song will it be?"

The mention of her name was enough to gather all these people and make them eager to listen. She truly was an amazing woman.

Aria should be like this, too, one day. I have to make that happen.

I sighed quietly. If I were to do that, the first thing I had to do was meet her and discuss the next steps. I started looking around for her.

"Where is she, anyway?"

"How are we supposed to find her in this crowd? Let's go to our seats first. She should be there." May pulled me after him as I searched for Aria.

Well, I guess she wouldn't have gotten separate seats for us if we were to watch it together. If I waited in my seat, she would no doubt appear with an awkward smile on her face.

"I haven't been to one of these in a long while. This is going to be fun." May seemed excited, regardless of how worried I was, as he took his seat. He'd claimed earlier that he was worried about Aria, too, but now he just seemed eager to see the performance.

I gave him a displeased look and sat down. The show would begin in thirty minutes. She had to come early if we were to converse at all beforehand. I stared anxiously at the unlit stage.

CHAPTER
ONE HUNDRED AND TWENTY-ONE

"Why isn't she coming?"

There were only five minutes remaining until the performance started. *She will not be able to come in once the performance begins...* I wondered what was taking her so long.

"They'll close the doors soon."

Should I go outside and look for her? I wondered. But May, who was sitting next to me, dissuaded me.

"There's no guarantee you'll find her even if you do. We're supposed to meet here, so I'm sure she'll be here after the performance."

He had a point. There were only three minutes left until the doors would shut. In the end, I decided to take May's advice and stay—just in case we failed to find each other outside.

"Ha..."

Moments later, the doors were closed, and the lights went out.

Thud.

The lights above the stage came on, and the audience clapped excitedly. But unlike the other people watching, I found it hard to concentrate. *I started all of this with good intentions because I truly enjoyed it. How did things end up like this?* Bitterly dwelling on such thoughts, I stared blankly at the stage, which danced with fancy lights.

The performance began, and Lady Priscilla's beautiful voice filled the air. The stage was decorated beautifully, the singing was sublime, and the performance was wonderfully composed. The stage was full of things to learn from, but I couldn't focus on them at all.

After Lady Priscilla, new singers, chorus members, and other people from her troupe came on stage, but all that meant for me was that someone else was singing again.

Quite some time passed until an urgent gesture from May forced me to take a closer look at the stage.

"Hey, did you know about this?"

"Know about what? Stop being so noisy..."

May shook me by the arm, and I finally saw what he was making such a fuss about. I nearly jumped to my feet at the sight in front of me.

"Are you nuts? Why are you trying to stand up?"

"Wait, am I seeing this right?"

It was Aria who stood on the stage.

"What in the world is going on?"

I couldn't remember anything about the performance that followed. Questions like why she was there and whether something had happened to my eyes floated around in my mind, making it impossible for me to think properly.

I wasn't the only one who was stunned. There were quite a few people who knew her in the audience. As soon as the curtains fell, noisy chatter sprang up everywhere.

"Wasn't that Lady Aria?"

"My goodness, I had no idea she was this good..."

"I heard that Lady Mary was investing in her, but to think she would perform at Lady Priscilla's concert! How did this happen?"

"Some called her an angel. I thought it was an exaggeration..."

I would normally have listened with some pride as people marveled and asked questions about her, but I didn't have the wherewithal for that today. Leaving May behind, I rushed out of the hall as soon as the performance ended.

"The manager."

"Pardon?"

"Call the manager of the theater. Right now." I needed someone to explain this situation to me, but I couldn't simply barge backstage. Anxiously, I grabbed a passing employee and demanded to see the manager.

"Are you Lady Mary?" said an employee who seemed to rank higher than the one I was speaking to.

"Do I know you?"

"Lady Aria is waiting for you. Please come this way." He led the way like he'd been waiting for me, and together we headed to the dressing room.

Thankfully, we got there without being crushed by the crowd because I was the only person who'd left the hall so quickly.

"This way." The man stopped in front of a small room.

Is Aria beyond this door? What should I say to her when we meet? Should I ask her how this came about or how long she's been in touch with Lady Priscilla? Or how long she has been preparing for this?

"Mary?"

I stood there for a while, trying to decide, but the door opened without giving me any time.

"Aria."

Aria, in elaborate stage makeup, was looking at me, one hand on the doorknob. She looked excited and awkward at the same time as she guided me in.

"Come inside."

She felt different as she led me into the dressing room. She couldn't have changed in such a short time, but why did she feel so different?

Of course, she had her hair done up nicely, her performance costume was ornate, and her face was covered with bold makeup that would make her stand out on the stage. But there was something else about her I couldn't quite explain.

"I have a few questions."

"Hahaha! I'm sure you do." Her laughter felt light and unburdened. She started to think as she sat in her chair. "Where do I begin...?"

"Have you been in touch with Lady Priscilla all this time?" I asked the most prominent question first.

Aria shook her head. "Not exactly. After the hunting competition, while you were lost in your worries, I tried to figure out what I could do on my own," she said calmly. "But there was nothing I could do alone. That was when I realized I needed to do something about it."

After the hunting competition, I'd realized that the story of the novel was having no impact on the world I currently lived in. Several days of labored thought had followed. I felt like I had taken up Aria's spot and ruined her future, and in that state, I was unable to focus on anything.

"So, I gave some thought to what I could do, even if it was something very small. Then it came to me. It was something Lady Priscilla had said."

When I heard her words, I was reminded of a remark Lady Priscilla had made in the past.

"If you don't mind, may I be Miss Aria's tutor?"

But that day had been a shock to Aria, and I thought that she would have wanted to forget about it.

"What she told me then wasn't easy to deal with at first, but I realized that it was natural for me to be lacking compared to other people."

"Lacking?!" I protested angrily.

Aria smiled. "But in hindsight, that wasn't something to be embarrassed about. It was natural, considering I had learned only briefly about singing and had very few opportunities compared to other people. What was really shameful was denying it and running away."

I composed myself after hearing Aria's comment. It was natural, of course, that Aria would have a less solid foundation than those who had been taught professionally, but I had not wanted to accept that. Someone I liked had to be perfect. And Aria was incredible in my eyes.

Apparently, Aria had thought differently.

"Nobody can be perfect without effort. And luckily for me, I had people willing to help," she said with a smile.

This was unbelievable, considering she'd thought of giving up when she was first told she wasn't good enough.

"I was nervous that Lady Priscilla might have changed her mind, but fortunately, she welcomed me with open arms," she said as she recalled the events of last month.

"This can't go on."

Aria had finally taken action on the second day Mary had closed herself up in her room. She wanted to do something to make up for the week or so that she had wasted like an idiot. But for some reason, Mary seemed upset and refused to leave her room, and Aria could do nothing without her.

This fact unnerved Aria. She had been aware that Mary had helped her greatly, but who knew her dependence on Mary had been so great? She felt very strongly that something needed to change.

"If there is anything I can do… anything at all…"

She considered this, and then a memory floated through her mind.

"Of course. The troupe won't give me too long a grace period, however, and I'd appreciate it if you'd let me know within two weeks."

Lady Priscilla had offered to teach her.

The two weeks had already passed, but Aria was incredibly desperate. The time she'd wasted already was too much for her to continue doing nothing.

For the first time in her life, she decided to follow her heart without thinking about the consequences.

"Lady Aria?" Lady Priscilla was surprised by the sudden visit, especially because Aria had come to her house instead of the theater or her personal performance hall.

"I fortunately remembered the address you gave me last time, so I just came."

"You should have written to me first. How long have you been waiting out here?"

"I'm not sure. Not that long," Aria said with a smile. This was a complete lie. She'd arrived when the sun had been high in the sky, but Lady Priscilla had returned around sunset.

"What is this about? No, first, come inside." Lady Priscilla guided her into the house. Unlike the ornate stages on which she performed, her house was plain, like an ordinary family home.

Moments later, she put down some tea on a simple table. "What is this about?"

"Lady Priscilla, I know that the two weeks you mentioned have already passed, and this might be too much to ask, but..." Aria took a deep breath.

What if she refuses? She realized she shouldn't have considered quitting like a fool and should have worked even harder. The initial offering had been an act of extreme kindness. *What if she thinks I'm a strange person because of this request?*

All sorts of worries filled Aria's brain, but she didn't want to back away.

"Could you teach me, please?" Aria decided she'd rather experience failure than tell herself nothing could be done. That way, she would not regret it when she looked back on this day when she was much older.

CHAPTER ONE HUNDRED AND TWENTY-TWO

"Could you teach me, please?"

Lady Priscilla blinked, startled by the determination in Aria's words.

There had been no letters from the marquess' mansion for over two weeks after her meeting with Aria. It was true that she had felt a little upset because Aria hadn't even bothered to notify her that she didn't want to be taught by Lady Priscilla. However, she hadn't been too surprised, considering how dumbfounded Aria had looked.

It was as if Aria's entire world had fallen apart at the first piece of negative criticism she had gotten, and perhaps she did not want to see Lady Priscilla again at all. This was why the current situation came as such a shock.

"It's far past the time you suggested, and I know that it's rude to come to you suddenly with this request," Aria said, doing her best to ignore how fast her heart was beating. "But I am too desperate to learn from you to let even the slightest opportunity go."

Aria had decided to let go of all her pride. If she could avoid living as a person who could do nothing on her own, her pride was not important.

"I understand what you mean," Lady Priscilla said after a pause.

Aria wondered what she would do if the lady refused. She waited anxiously for the answer.

"But I've started working again, you see…"

Thud.

It felt as if Aria's heart had plummeted to the ground. *I shouldn't have expected anything from the start—no, rather, I should have come to her sooner.* She bit her lip, berating herself for her foolishness.

What do I do now? She wanted to avoid becoming an idiot who had to depend on others to accomplish anything.

"It may be difficult to put together a schedule, but we can arrange it if you'd like."

Aria could not believe her ears. She blinked. *Did I just hear her right? Does this mean…*

"You mean to say that you will teach me?"

"Yes." Lady Priscilla answered with a nod. There was a reason she agreed to teach Aria despite her hectic schedule. Firstly, Aria had great talent. Lady Priscilla had seen many singers, after becoming the head singer of a troupe and the greatest prima donna in the empire, and she'd witnessed many singers-in-training perform. None had been as talented as Aria. No one who had the slightest interest in teaching someone their craft would have been able to avoid feeling this way about Aria.

And there was something about the girl that caught her eye. She seemed to have the potential to achieve what Lady Priscilla wanted—to please both herself and the audience with her music.

"You are passionate and gifted. I have no reason not to teach a student like you."

And from the way Aria had been waiting in front of her home with no idea when she would return, it was clear there had been some marked change in the girl's mindset. It wasn't clear what that change was, but it was no doubt a positive one that would change her life.

"Thank you," Aria said, relaxing into a smile. Aria knew that just because she could learn from Lady Priscilla and because she'd done something without Mary's help, it did not mean she was a completely different person now. But she had taken the most important first step, and she felt invincible. "I'll try my best not to let you down."

"Oh my, I have no reason to be disappointed in you. All I ask is that you never be disappointed in yourself."

Lady Priscilla smiled back at her, and so their secret lessons began.

"So, all this time you've been leaving the mansion…"

"I was getting lessons from Lady Priscilla. I'm sorry I didn't tell you before."

I had wondered where she was going all those times. She was meeting with Lady Priscilla. I felt touched to think she had been trying so hard without me, like I was a mother watching my child grow up.

"Were you at Lady Priscilla's house the last few days, then?"

"After what Lady Iris said, I thought about a lot of things."

I wondered if she was talking about how Iris had said Aria could say nothing if I wasn't around. Frowning, I listened to her speak.

"Her actions and words were rude and malicious… but there was one thing I had to agree with."

"But nobody can do everything on their own. You don't have to worry about anything she said."

"You have a point, but I got the feeling I would start depending on you for everything, even the small things, if things went on the way they were," Aria said, shaking her head gently. "I wanted to be helpful to you and be unashamed of my own behavior."

That really wasn't necessary, but I didn't say this out loud. I was already catching on to the fact that some huge change had occurred inside her.

"When Lady Priscilla first suggested I perform on stage, I was going to refuse, thinking it was too early for that. But what Baron Robert said reminded me of something Lady Priscilla had told me before."

What Baron Robert said... I was sure Aria was referring to what he said about not being able to place a singer with no experience on his stage.

"The thought that I could finally achieve something without your help made me feel that I needed to work harder." Aria laughed, covering her mouth. "I'm sorry I didn't tell you sooner. Frankly, I wanted to surprise you."

"If that was your goal, you certainly succeeded with flying colors." I'd really had no idea. She had invited me to a performance, and I'd assumed I would watch it with her, not see her on the stage. She had outdone herself onstage, just as I'd expected.

Aria seemed to have been born for a beautiful stage and the applause of a crowd. Though it was her first time performing on such a large stage, she seemed right at home.

"This will satisfy Baron Robert's demand, at least, so please forgive me," she said, laughing playfully.

As she'd said, even the inflexible Baron Robert would have to admit this was a notable accomplishment. If he claimed that a singer who had performed solo at Lady Priscilla's performance was a nobody, then no one in that troupe would be worthy.

"But still, you should tell me next time. I was so surprised, you know. If it hadn't been for May, I might have shot out of my seat right there..."

Oops. I completely forgot about May. I smiled awkwardly, recalling how I had left him in his seat. *Well, he's no child. He isn't the sort to wait for me either, so he probably went home already.* I nodded to myself as I justified my actions.

"Lord May? You came with him?" Aria's eyes widened.

"L-Lord Ethen said he was busy, so I had no choice but to bring him. He had nothing else to do," I stammered, lying about Ethen. The truth was that I hadn't asked him about it or told him that I was going to this performance.

"Lord Ethen refused to come? He must have been really busy. You must've been disappointed."

"He has things to take care of, and I'm no child to be disappointed over something like that." I did my best to sound nonchalant.

"Still, I thought Lord Ethen would come with you no matter what if you asked." Aria's innocent comments pricked my conscience.

"Maybe... yes. Anyway, sometimes we have important things we can't set aside," I said, biting my lip softly.

"I suppose." Aria smiled casually. "You'll have plenty more time to spend together, anyway. I suppose it's fine."

I simply smiled at her without saying anything.

"Anyway, now that this performance is over, I feel really carefree."

As she said, Aria looked completely free of worry or concern, unlike usual. It was as if she had shaken off everything that had been bothering her.

"You really were amazing today. Everyone else was astonished as well. Though that's not too surprising considering I'm the one who saw your potential." I changed the subject, trying my best not to think about Ethen.

I'd been so astounded that I wasn't able to watch the crowd in detail, but even so, I had noticed how impressed everyone was. And this was Lady Priscilla's performance, of all places, so Aria's skill would be talked about far and wide, and she'd become even more famous.

"The stage lights were so bright; I couldn't see the crowd very well. I'm relieved to hear you say that."

"I don't like the fact that you kept this a secret from me, but we should get back and celebrate, don't you think?"

There was no reason not to celebrate. Aria would be able to perform at the imperial theater as a lead singer, and it would only be a matter of time before Edville fell for her.

I can't give up now if I want to make that happen.

"Right. I think I can leave early after I say goodbye to Lady Priscilla. You said Lord May came with you, so we can go back with him," Aria said, beaming.

Uh, I don't actually know where May is.

"I sent him home alone, so he's probably gone already," I lied again, then changed the subject. "Where is Lady Priscilla? It was nice hearing her sing again. Haha." I felt sorry because I had asked May to come and then abandoned him, but he would be all right. "I'm sure my parents will be happy to see you as well."

I smiled, pretending that everything was fine.

CHAPTER
ONE HUNDRED
AND TWENTY-THREE

"Are you kidding me?"

Contrary to my assumption that he would have left without a second thought, I found May waiting for me in front of the performance hall.

"I thought you said he'd left," Aria said.

"Hahaha! That's what I thought. What is he doing here? I have no idea," I said with an embarrassed smile. I thought he'd left. *Why is he still here?*

"I waited out front because I was afraid to move and miss you."

Since when were you so thoughtful?

"Lady Aria, your performance today was amazing," he said, walking past me. Aria was in her everyday dress, but there was still some of her stage makeup on her face. She smiled shyly.

"Thank you."

"My parents wanted to hear you sing as well. It would have been great if they could have come, too."

They began what appeared to be a friendly conversation. But I still had a lot to discuss with Aria, and I didn't really like her speaking with anyone who wasn't a male lead from the novel, so I cut their conversation short and got onto the carriage.

"Let's get back. We should have some champagne and celebrate."

"You're right. Today is a special day for Lady Aria," May said, escorting Aria onto the carriage.

And just like that, Aria's short time away from the mansion came to an end.

"My goodness, we would have gone to the performance if we had known!"

"I failed to think of it. I'll make sure to invite you next time."

That evening, a small party was held to celebrate Aria's theater debut. May had asked for the key to the wine cellar, saying that we needed to celebrate a day like this with good wine, but my father said that wine was not enough and instead hurriedly threw together a party. My family and Aria were the only people present, but the mood was as festive as any party.

"To think you would perform at one of Lady Priscilla's concerts! And what's more, you're being taught by her! I didn't realize we had such an amazing guest staying at our mansion."

"You're right. The Imperial Opera Theater will be opening its doors soon, so I guess we'll be able to hear you sing soon enough, I suppose. I'm looking forward to it already."

My mother and father continued to compliment Aria and smile at her. They were happy for her, of course, but they also seemed happy that my foul mood, which had lasted several days, had finally lifted a little.

"You'll have the best seats when that happens," I said, smiling along and clinking glasses with my family.

"I never thought I would ever get to perform on such an amazing stage. It's all thanks to Mary," Aria said.

"Of course it's thanks to me. But if you hadn't had the talent, not even I would have been able to put you on the stage."

And to be honest, I had nothing to do with her performing on Lady Priscilla's stage today. I decided to praise her some more.

"Lady Priscilla happened to hear Aria sing once, and she said she wanted to teach her. It just goes to show how right I was about her."

"Is this true?" my mother asked, her eyes wide.

Aria blushed and nodded. "Yes."

"Goodness me, Mary. You must have a great eye for these things," my mother said, looking at me proudly.

My father also looked overwhelmed as he cleared his throat. "Ahem. I thought it was absurd at first when you said you would invest in a singer... I guess I was wrong. I wasn't aware my daughter was this clever and talented."

As my doting parents watched me with tears in their eyes, I felt moved myself. Turning away to hide my emotions, I said, "Haha. Of course. I'm your daughter, aren't I?"

"I thought we'd be lucky if she didn't get into more trouble. She seems to have become a bit more sensible now, which is a relief," May interjected, ruining the mood. But even this was a huge improvement, considering how much he'd suffered because of Mary.

"I've learned and gained so much since Mary came into my life." Aria continued to sing my praises. "She allowed me to start singing and performing on stage, but I also learned a lot from spending time with her."

"Mary also changed a lot after meeting you, Lady Aria. You are like family to us now," my mother said with a smile.

Family. My mother must have heard what happened at the duchess' party. If she was still saying this, it probably meant she really liked Aria.

"We'd love it if you stayed in the mansion with us forever... but I suppose that might be difficult as you have your own life to live."

"I'm grateful that you would suggest it at all."

"Oh, but I meant it."

It felt nice to be sitting amid such pleasant conversation for a change. There was still so much left to be done, and this was probably not even a tiny portion of the happiness that Aria deserved. *But perhaps I can afford to relax and smile for a day.*

"What are you saying?" I said. "By next year, she'll be so famous that everyone in the empire will recognize her. She probably won't even have time to come home."

"Oh my. I think you're right," my mother said, her eyes widening as she clapped her hands together. "I'm going to brag to my friends that Lady Aria is close friends with my daughter," she said, laughing like a young girl.

"Please tell us if you need our help with anything. Admittedly, we don't know much about the field... but we'll do what we can," my father said kindly.

"If I do need help with anything, I'll be sure to ask you. Hearing that makes me feel so encouraged."

"Haha. That's good. You've got nothing to fear since you've taken a great first step." My father raised his glass. The transparent wine that he had set aside for a special occasion glittered in the light. "Why don't we make a toast to the great things to come?"

We all raised our glasses and walked over to him. With a toast from him, our glasses clinked.

"To progress, for all of us!"

"Cheers!"

I had always hated parties, but I realized that they could be pleasant when they were with the right people. It seemed like only yesterday that I had complained about parties in this world, but now I was enjoying one.

I guess I've gotten quite used to this world. I smiled softly.

My father, mother, and May picked up after themselves and went inside, and Aria and I spent some more time together in the garden. As we talked, sipping our wine, we soon ran out of it. Not wanting the moment to end just yet, I quietly called Lilian.

"Yes, my lady."

"Go bring another bottle of this."

"I'm sorry, my lady, but this is from the master's special collection. There is no other bottle like it."

Oh, right. Remembering this, I licked my lips. But there was still more to talk about, and I didn't want to go inside yet.

"Would you like me to bring a different wine?"

"Yes. It doesn't have to be as expensive as this one. Just make sure it's good enough."

"Yes, my lady," Lilian said, and she went into the mansion. I stared up at the stars, sitting beside Aria on a bench.

"How were Lady Priscilla's lessons?"

"Uhm... there were some points I had never thought of, which was interesting."

"Have you met other people as well?"

"Not very many, but she did introduce me to a few trustworthy people."

We spent time making small talk. She had been away only three days and performed just once, but something about her seemed completely different. Trying to shake the feeling of awkwardness, I started to ramble to keep the conversation going.

"It would have been nice if Baron Robert had been there. I bet he would have been shocked and regretted the harsh treatment he gave you."

"I doubt it."

"I'm very curious how he'll react now. He must have heard about your performance." I felt a bit more relaxed now that Aria had achieved something to show the baron.

We'll be able to confidently put forth our opinions regarding the performances and the theater. And that will mean more frequent meetings between Aria and Edville, and that in turn—

"My lady."

Whoa.

It was Lilian who interrupted my thoughts. As requested, she'd brought a new bottle of wine and two glasses.

"I brought the best one I could find."

There was a problem, though. It wasn't really a problem, but it bothered me somewhat.

"It's red wine," I commented.

I had avoided coming to be on bad terms with Aria, but red wine still brought back memories of a certain celebration—the way red wine had splattered over a white dress and how damp my dress had felt on my skin.

And as it happened, Aria was wearing a white dress again today.

"Is there a problem, my lady?" Lilian asked carefully.

In the past, I would have screamed at her to get rid of the wine the moment I saw it, but today I felt more easygoing.

"No, it's nothing." I held the glasses up for Lilian to fill. Dark red wine swished about in my glass, and I tilted it slightly, watching the liquid inside.

"Come to think of it, it was red wine that brought us together, wasn't it?" Aria said.

I started to cough in surprise. It was a good thing I didn't have any wine in my mouth because I would have spewed it out.

"You remember that?" I asked.

"How could I forget?"

Is it as hard to forget for her as it is for me? I sipped my wine and listened to her speak.

CHAPTER ONE HUNDRED AND TWENTY-FOUR

"It was my first party. Even choosing the dress was difficult, and the imperial palace was a very bewildering and maze-like place," Aria said, gazing afar with her glass in her hand.

"I had no one to follow, so I had lost my way. Thankfully, Lord Vante helped me find my way to the banquet hall, but that didn't make things much easier."

"You seemed quite comfortable, for all that."

"Hahaha! I responded to everyone who spoke to me, and time flew by quickly," she said, recalling the events of that day. "Even before I bumped into you, I found you very impressive, Mary."

"Why?"

"Well, you looked... confident. You sparkled in that crowd. That's what I thought about you."

All I had done was avoid Aria with a passion, wanting to be free of the situation. I had no idea she had seen me that way. Embarrassed, I gulped my wine.

"Of course. That's the sort of person I am." My self-control seemed to be slipping because of the wine.

"And what's more, I made a huge mistake that day."

She was probably talking about how she had spilled wine over my dress. I shuddered as I recalled the incident. At that point, I believed that the story of the novel still held sway over this world, but my blind trust in that betrayed me later.

"I simply couldn't think. I wondered if I was bound to always make trouble wherever I went, incapable of doing anything on my own. It made me second-guess myself and wonder if my father had been right. It was your words, Mary, that helped me relax."

"Did you think I'd forgive you just because you're crying in such a pretty way?"

It really wasn't something someone would expect to hear under such circumstances. The only problem was that she probably felt not so much relieved as perplexed.

"I was a bit taken aback, to be honest, but it helped banish my gloomy thoughts," Aria said, stifling her laughter. "I was shocked at first, but I wasn't able to say anything after His Majesty showed up. You handled the situation for me beautifully, and I thought you were amazing."

"Haha. Of course I am," I said, blushing because of the alcohol.

"I wanted to become friends with you, and you have no idea how happy I was when you offered to gift me a dress. Oh, it wasn't the dress I was happy about—"

"Yes, I know. You were happy that you would get to see me again."

It wasn't surprising she had been touched by the slightest of kind gestures, because living with Edward had caused her self-esteem to plummet. My gesture, however, had been odd rather than kind.

"Yes. And the way I sang in front of you that day… I think something came over me. I wasn't a brave enough person to sing to anyone in public."

Of course you weren't. Aria had been fated to sing that day, even if I hadn't been with her—the day was supposed to have changed her life. She would have gotten to know Edville instead of me, and they would have grown interested in each other.

"I think the heavens must have given me the courage to grab a once-in-a-lifetime opportunity."

That courage wasn't meant to be used on me. My heart ached with guilt more and more as I listened.

"Something else also happened that day," I said. Maybe it was the wine I kept drinking, but I said something I would have never said in my right mind. Completely red in the face, I revealed my innermost thoughts little by little.

"What? Uhm..." she said, thinking for a moment and smiling at me awkwardly. "What else was there? Meeting you left such a deep impression, I can't remember anything else," She had apparently forgotten that she'd met Edville that day.

"You don't remember meeting the Crown Prince that day?"

"Oh, right," she said, finally remembering and clapping her hands. "Back then I thought that we might become friends one day, but I guess you never know with people."

"Why? You could have become friends with him if you hadn't met me, don't you think?"

"Do you think so?" Aria tilted her head. "Hmm, I suppose you might be right. You can never predict these things."

What if I told you that it was your fate? What if I told you that despite all the things you might have gone through after meeting Edville, you'd win out in the end and become his wife?

Would Aria treat me the same way if she found out?

"Don't you feel disappointed?"

"What do you mean?"

"If you'd become friends with him back then, you might be lovers right now, who knows?"

Aria blinked as I spoiled the plot of the novel. She stared at me as if she could never even imagine such a thing and then burst out laughing.

"Hahaha! That sounds like something straight out of a novel. Me, the wife of the Crown Prince? That's absurd."

"Why? I can imagine it happening," I said in a serious voice. Aria seemed to notice something odd and stopped laughing. She had realized that I wasn't simply entertaining wishful fantasies here, though she probably didn't know what I was trying to get at.

"That doesn't seem likely, but if it had happened, I guess it would have been remarkable."

"Of course. You would have become the most powerful woman in the empire. And if you had, people like Lady Iris and Lady Zir would not have dared to treat you the way they did," I said in a serious, frustrated tone. If she'd been his wife—no, even just his lover—they would not have behaved like that toward her. In the novel, the only women picking on Aria were me, Ashley, and Maia. But now there were a bunch of women doing their best to harass her at every opportunity.

"They're weaklings who've never accomplished a single thing on their own, and the only thing they've got going for them is their family backgrounds..." I spat angrily, completely drunk. I spun around to look at her. "Don't they annoy you?"

Aria seemed to think for a moment, noticing that I wanted her agreement. After debating what to say, she answered, "I've felt upset about it, yes."

"That would have never happened if you had become his wife..."

It seemed the new wine was much stronger than the one I'd shared with my family. *Why else would I be rambling on like this?*

"That day... if I hadn't asked you to sing and just left you alone, you would have become friends with His Highness. Do you know that?"

"Pardon?" Aria looked completely baffled. "I think you've had too much wine. Why don't we go inside now?"

"No, Aria. You have no idea." My inhibitions were gone, and despite the awkward atmosphere, the words tumbled out of my mouth uncontrollably. "Life may be unpredictable, but I didn't know this would happen."

"Mary, you're drunk..."

"It's supposed to be a happy ending for the two of you..."

The story was no fairy tale, but a book was a book. It was clear that the two main characters falling in love and living happily ever after would have been the best ending of all.

"I'm already happy as it is. Why are you saying that?"

"Of course you are. I made sure of that."

I knew that Aria had no problems with her current life. She took pride in her work and loved performing in front of others. That didn't mean I felt comfortable, though. I still imagined the perfect ending she could have had if I hadn't entered this world.

"But you might have been happier still had you chosen a different path. For example, as the Crown Prince's lover..."

"Mary," Aria said in a voice I'd never heard from her before. She seemed angry for some reason as she stared right into my eyes. "Why are you saying this?"

"What do you mean?" I said, drunk and feeling hurt by how cold she sounded. She'd never spoken to me like that before, but she seemed really upset as she looked straight at me.

"I could not be happier with the life I have now. Happiness doesn't come solely from relationships or marriage."

"But the Crown Prince—"

"All right, it makes no sense whatsoever, but let's assume that he and I had started a relationship after that day," she said, cutting me off. "Do you think I'd be happier than I am right now if that had happened?"

"Who wouldn't be after marrying the man she loved and becoming the wife of the Crown Prince?" I said, pouting. I knew in my head that Aria wouldn't understand my meaning, but I couldn't seem to stop myself. "That's how it is in the fairy tales and the novels."

"I'm not some character from a novel, Mary."

Actually, you are. I shook my head. "You have no idea, Aria—"

"What do you mean, I have no idea?" she said, sounding even more angry.

"In this world," I said evenly, "social status is what matters most. You may find happiness in other things, but you've missed the biggest opportunity of your life. How can you not feel disappointed?"

"I have no idea what you're trying to say right now, Mary."

Of course she didn't. I wouldn't have been able to accept it either if I'd been living life just fine and someone appeared out of the blue, claiming something had prevented me from reaching complete happiness.

"Let's assume, purely for argument's sake, that I *was* fated to marry him. Why should you feel guilty about that?"

"Because you missed an opportunity to be happier..."

"Happier... Mary, you're a good person and my friend, but you don't have to feel responsible for my life," she said firmly. "I'm not someone you need to care for. I'm just me. And I finally know now where my happiness lies."

I was speechless.

"I'm not a character in a novel. I'm just an ordinary person living in the real world."

Her words were diametrically opposed to everything I'd believed so far.

ONE HUNDRED AND TWENTY-FIVE

"I'm not a character in a novel. I'm just an ordinary person living in the real world," Aria said, her voice firm. She was upset, as if I had insulted her. "Mary, you are not my mother or anyone who is responsible for me."

"What do you know, Aria? I know much more than anyone else does. That's why I can't help but feel concerned," I shot back, growing angrier still. She was a good person, a good friend, and someone who deserved to shine. But I knew that this whole world belonged in a novel. "Everyone has a place in life decided for them."

"Are you serious?" Aria said, looking right into my eyes. Only then did I realize that I might have sounded just like Lady Iris or Lady Zir, disparaging her status, and cut myself short.

"In any case... don't you feel disappointed in the least?"

"Of course I don't."

"Why not?" I couldn't understand her. This world was inside a romance novel. Surely love was of the greatest value here, and its fulfillment was the only way that the story could come to a happy ending. *How could Aria be so convinced?*

"I have no feelings for His Highness whatsoever. And even if I were to fall in love with him, I know that I'd love my work even more. That I'm sure of."

"How can you be so sure? You haven't experienced it yet."

"I already have many things I love," she said in a confident voice. "I love the opportunities I am given, singing in front of a crowd, being the object of admiration and applause, and the fact that I am capable of accomplishing all of it on my own."

Her eyes sparkled as she spoke. It was hard to believe that this was the same Aria as when I'd first met her—shy and unable to trust herself.

"And you're the person who taught me all this, Mary. So why do you speak as if you know nothing of these things and the happiness they bring?"

To be sure, I was the person who had awakened her to the joy of singing and her dormant desire to perform in front of people.

"Do you think you've become happy because I've taught you those things?" I asked, my voice trembling.

"Yes," she replied without a moment's hesitation. She took my hand. "I don't know why you're thinking like this, but I'm happy. I'm glad that I can do something, and every single day is an exciting adventure."

Would she be able to enjoy eternal happiness even if she didn't get to be the female lead of the novel?

"Do you think that happiness will last forever?"

"There will be rough days, that's for sure. Some days I'll want to quit, and some days I'll feel like running away."

But that's not good. I unconsciously frowned at her.

"But that's what it means to live." She didn't seem to fear the hardships that might lie ahead of her. "There will be difficulties, but hope will allow me to get up again each time I fall."

I blinked at her. *When did she become such a hopeful person?*

"I know where my happiness lies, and I know I'm capable of getting back up. I'm not afraid of anything anymore," Aria said with a smile. "I'm always grateful to you, Mary, since you're the person who taught me that I can be like this."

She's grateful to me? I wondered if I deserved to hear such a thing. I hung my head, red in the face, and muttered, "Does that mean..."

"Mary, you don't have to think you need to take care of me. You might think me impudent, but there is only one thing I want from you. I want you to be happy. I don't know what will make you happy, but I want you to have a happy life, making no sacrifices for other people, and certainly not feeling guilty toward me. I'll become a person worthy of your friendship, so all you need to do is stay friends with me."

In the novel, Aria was an amazing person, a person who lived for love. As was common in romance novels, she was shy but also brave, capable of doing rash things for love. The Aria in front of me, however, seemed to be living for something else. She loved singing and her work.

Whenever she seemed uninterested in Edville or the other potential male leads, I assumed that she simply hadn't become aware of her own fate and didn't know herself well enough. My assumption was that the future was set, and that love would be her greatest value because she was the female lead.

But I realized now that I'd been the one who'd been in the dark.

She was not merely a character in a book. In this world, she was very much alive. And I was not someone who was duty bound to adhere to the story.

I was also just another ordinary person, living in this world with no guilt or burden. I was completely ordinary, with the exception of my wicked tongue.

"Stop saying such silly things. Of course I'll stay your friend." I laughed, realizing just how long—and how many glasses of wine—it had taken me to understand this.

"Ugh... my head..."

I woke up at noon. My head felt like it was splitting apart, and I had fallen asleep without changing out of my clothes. I felt stiff and cramped all over.

"Ouch... What did I do yesterday?"

"You have no idea, Aria—"

Hands on my aching head, I thought about yesterday's events for a moment. I froze as the memories came back.

"What do you know, Aria? I know much more than anyone else does. That's why I can't help but feel concerned."

"Do you think that happiness will last forever?"

What the hell? What did I say to her yesterday? I kicked at my sheets and cursed myself for what I had done. Still, I'd gained something from the conversation.

After kicking at the sheets some more, absolutely mortified, I stopped and stared out the window. Yesterday's conversation hadn't just been a drunken memory that was better off forgotten. My brain was still foggy, but I had realized a lot of things through last night's talk.

Aria was not some unfortunate female lead that I needed to protect and care for. She had experienced so much change without me knowing it, and I knew now that it would be a terrible waste to spend time dwelling on my stupid guilt.

"I know where my happiness lies, and I know I'm capable of getting back up. I'm not afraid of anything anymore."

If she was capable of saying that, Aria would find her place on her own without my having to worry about her.

"My head..."

I tried to drift into some emotional thought, but my headache got in the way. I tried to remember what I did after the conversation. I rummaged through my blurry memories and finally managed to remember.

"So, I know he likes me, but I'm not sure if I'm allowed to return his feelings!"

I froze when a scene floated across my brain. After the conversation, I'd immersed myself in the mood and had even more to drink, although Aria had tried to stop me. At a certain point, I'd grown so tipsy that...

"Why do I have to be so popular? It's always the people I want nothing to do with that are attracted to me."

"I thought you liked Lord Ethen?"

"Well, yes, I do like him, but..."

Damn it, did I really say that? What was worse was that I couldn't really remember the rest of it. *What did I do?* I was sitting with my hands on my head when someone knocked.

"My lady, it's Lilian."

"Come in," I managed to rasp.

Lilian walked in with a teapot and a cup on a tray. "This tea will help with your hangover. Would you like some?"

"Yes. Quick."

No doubt Aria and Lilian had gotten me to my room after I'd become roaring drunk. Clearing my throat awkwardly, I took a sip of the tea.

"About yesterday... I can't seem to remember. What time did I return to my room?"

"Close to midnight."

I remembered seeing the clock strike ten last night. That meant I'd been in a drunken daze for another two hours afterward.

Sipping again, I said, "I slept in my clothes. I nearly died of cramp."

"My apologies, my lady. I tried to help you change out of your clothes, but you didn't like being touched. We had no choice but to remove only your accessories."

"Everyone out!"

I seemed to remember more of last night after hearing Lilian's words.

"I'm sleepy! I'm not changing!"

"My lady, if you sleep in those clothes—"

"Whatever! Don't you dare touch me! Begone!"

I hadn't known I was such a mean drunk. Clamping my eyes shut, I resolved to never drink that much again. *I know my limit now.*

"You know what? Forget I mentioned it."

Sorry you had to see that. I apologized inwardly and drank some more tea.

"What about Aria?"

"She left early in the morning. She said she had a class to attend."

Why is Aria so unaffected by the alcohol? I realized that Aria had mostly just held her cup in her hand without actually drinking from it. I, on the other hand, had gulped down the wine whenever I felt the slightest bit of frustration. Perhaps this was a natural result.

"Did she say when she would be back?"

"A little past lunchtime, my lady."

I turned and looked at the clock. It was just past twelve, so she would be back in a couple of hours.

"Have a carriage ready. We're going to the imperial theater as soon as she returns. And did you check on the thing I asked you about?"

"Yes, my lady. I sent someone to check early in the morning, as you instructed, and they found it."

"All right. Tell them to leave that on my table. Help me get dressed."

I got up, feeling stiff all over. Baron Robert had told us to show him our actual achievements, but he probably hadn't thought we would achieve so much so quickly. I was excited at the prospect of seeing the shock on his face.

With a grin, I tidied my messy hair.

CHAPTER
ONE HUNDRED AND TWENTY-SIX

"Are you sure it's a good idea to go so quickly?"

"Of course."

Aria seemed dazed by the fact that I had suggested we leave so soon after she got back, but I hurried her along without any worry.

"It's already too late if we really want to prepare thoroughly."

Baron Robert had demanded that we accomplish something meaningful before the theater opened its doors. There were fewer than two months remaining until that date, and we had to speak to him as soon as possible if we were to decide on a new direction for the performance that included Aria.

"But the performance was just yesterday. Even if rumors are quick, he might not know about it yet."

"It's stupid to worry about such things. You don't think I thought of that?" I said, confidently resting a hand on the table. "See? I've got everything ready."

I'd had Lilian bring a pile of newspapers that had been printed today and had organized all the articles about Aria.

"What's this?"

"Read them," I said proudly, pushing the papers toward her. She looked flabbergasted as she read one.

"There are articles about me?"

"It's nothing surprising. A new singer has appeared in one of Lady Priscilla's performances, and as it turns out, she's the angel everyone's been talking about. Of course you drew a lot of attention." I tapped the desk triumphantly.

"So, all of this is…"

"You're the talk of the capital right now. Some papers even had you on the front page," I said, shrugging.

Aria looked over the desk and read the other articles as well. "Oh." A few letters fell off the desk, pushed off by the papers that covered it.

"I'm sorry. I'll get those out of the way."

What are those letters again? I froze for a moment as Aria bent down to pick them up.

"Wait, these are…"

The letters were all marked with the seal of the duke's house. *Oops. I put those on the desk, didn't I?* Belatedly realizing what they were, I tried to snatch them away. But it was too late.

"These are from the duke's house. Why didn't you even open them?"

I took the letters from her and hid them behind my back. "I was going to read all of them at once."

"There are so many of them..." Aria said, looking at me suspiciously.

I'd forgotten about leaving the letters on the table. Belatedly regretting my thoughtlessness, I fidgeted with my hands behind my back. "I was... busy."

"But you weren't so busy that you couldn't have read Lord Ethen's letters. Did something happen between you two?"

Not just something. I turned my eyes away. "I was busy, and I had a lot of things to think about. That's not important right now. I asked for a carriage, so we'll probably have to leave soon."

The letters I hadn't read but hadn't been able to throw away were placed back on the desk. Aria continued to look dubiously at them, but I ignored her and pulled her out of the room.

There were only two months left until the Imperial Opera Theater opened its doors. That being the case, the construction work on both the exterior and interior of the building seemed to be nearing its end.

"The construction will be completed by next month at the latest. And we'll be announcing the building's purpose to the public a month before the opening," an employee said proudly as he guided us. "We're very excited to see how surprised people will be. I used to run a theater in a large tourist city, though it was not as big as the capital. No matter how much I advertised the place and tried to make it work, it couldn't compare to theaters here."

The employee continued his chatter, apparently having a lot to say on the subject. "But now that I work here, I'm very happy because I can be proud of my job. I'm also honored to meet you, Lady Aria. People call you the 'Angel of the Streets,' I know." He spun to face her. "I would have loved to have been there at the performance yesterday. You have no idea how surprised I was to hear the news. The baron seemed taken aback as well, though he didn't say anything."

I perked up my ears, wondering how that inflexible man had reacted. "What was his reaction?"

"His eyes went wide instantly. Now, I haven't known him for that long, but he's always been the gruff and reticent sort. Seeing him like that reminded me that he is also human and prone to human emotions," he said with a chuckle.

I'd brought the newspapers in case the baron hadn't heard Aria's news yet, but perhaps it had been unnecessary. I went to see Baron Robert with a confident look on my face.

"Lady Mary Bell and Lady Aria Peridot have come to see you," the employee said, knocking on the baron's door.

I walked in with a spring in my step. "Nice to see you again."

"Yes."

It hadn't actually been that long, but I tried to sound as arrogant as possible. "I wonder how the opening preparations have been going? I hope you haven't made that much progress." I laughed with my mouth partially covered. "You'll have to revise the entire plan for the performance, after all. You won't be so underhanded as to go back on your word, will you?" I said gloatingly.

Baron Robert adjusted his glasses. "No, we haven't made that much progress yet, thankfully."

Feeling like I'd gotten one up on this proud man, a sense of victory came over me. "Then no more words will be necessary."

"We were only beginning to plan for the performance, so you have nothing to worry about. But we are very short on time, so we'd like you to start taking part in the rehearsals with the other members of the troupe as soon as you can— even tomorrow, if possible."

You're telling us that a little too late, don't you think? Were you planning to put her on stage without any rehearsal all this time?

A little upset, I stared him right in the face. "I wonder why there is so little time."

"Lady Aria is not a member of this troupe, but someone sponsored by you, Lady Mary. So, her schedule may differ slightly from that of the others, but I will try to make it as convenient as possible," the baron said, subtly making it clear that Aria was not technically part of the troupe.

"There's no need." It was Aria who answered him. With a smile and a polite tone, she said, "Even if I don't belong to the troupe, I will be working on the performance along with everyone else."

"But we are not your employer, Lady Aria—"

"I don't care about that. I'd like to learn, rehearse, and prepare in the exact same way," she said with a smile, not backing up a single inch. "I don't mind if we start tomorrow or even today. I'm excited by the prospect of meeting the members I'll be working with."

"All right... I'll take note of that. Aer, show Lady Aria where the rehearsal room is and explain the schedule to her."

"Yes, my lord," said the employee who guided us here. "I'm sure they'll be glad to see you. Hahaha," Aer said to Aria, chuckling insensitively as the baron frowned.

His cluelessness wasn't such a bad thing for us.

"I'd like to bring you some tea and sit down with you for a while, but I don't think that'll be possible, considering we'll have to revise our plans for the performance today."

"Oh... of course you're busy. Haha!" I said provokingly. I glanced at the baron, who was sighing quietly with a complicated expression on his face. "Since you're busy, we'll take our leave. You said this man would show us around?"

"Yes..."

"See you again soon," I said annoyingly before leaving the room with Aer and Aria.

"Oh, I should show you the rehearsal room first," said the eager but tactless employee. "I don't think it'll be possible for you to join the others today, but I'll make sure you can tomorrow," he said, his eyes glowing. "Some of them can be a little sensitive, but most of them are good-natured people. I'm sure you'll have no trouble fitting right in."

With the cheerful Aer as our guide, we checked the location of the rehearsal room and were told about tomorrow's schedule. The vague anxiety I'd been feeling finally wore off, and I was able to leave the theater in a state of excitement.

"Looks like the papers weren't necessary. I was going to push them in that old man's face," I said, glancing at the papers I'd kept in the carriage as we rode home. "The articles were so nice, too. What a pity." I snickered as I looked at the articles.

Aria picked up a paper and started reading it. "Fascinating. Me, talked about in the papers? I never imagined such a thing was possible."

"Even more outrageous things are bound to happen. You can't be dumbfounded already. By the way, you'll be a lot busier starting tomorrow, won't you?" I said, thinking of the schedule Aer had described. There was only about a month and a half left until the performance, which was not a lot by any means. "Tell me if anyone is unfriendly toward you. I'll go teach them a lesson," I said with a grin.

"It's all right. Life is full of both good and bad things. If I run into a problem, I want to take care of it. I'll be fine," Aria said confidently.

I looked at her fondly, wondering if this was how it felt to have one's child grow into an adult.

"You've got your own things to deal with. I can't keep you occupied with mine. It's only right that I do what I can by myself."

"This is what I've chosen to spend my time on, you know. And I'm not so weak that I can't deal with being a bit busy," I said, running a hand through my hair.

Aria looked at me oddly. "I don't think you're quite right about that."

I gazed at her in surprise. She seemed to have something to say.

"Is there something you think I should be doing, then?" I didn't have to study to continue the family business like May did, and I had no work of my own to do. I looked at her in confusion.

"Those letters earlier were all from Lord Ethen. Why didn't you even open them?" she asked, looking right into my eyes.

CHAPTER
ONE HUNDRED AND TWENTY-SEVEN

This is the moment I've been dreading. I gulped, tensing at the question.

"I'm not sure what you mean," I said, turning away.

As expected, Aria caught on to my little act and said in a serious voice, "Even if you have a million things to think about, it's not right that you haven't been paying attention to the important things because you were busy on my account."

I bit my lip gently, feeling as if she was scolding me.

While I no longer felt duty bound to turn her into the female lead that I knew, this was a different matter. I couldn't tell Ethen that we should continue our relationship because I felt comfortable with it again, and even if I chose to approach him, I wasn't sure how to go about it. It had always been him who approached me first.

Those damned letters. I would have liked nothing more than to throw them out.

"It's not that important. Don't worry about it." In the end, I ended up lying to her as I searched for an excuse.

"Why? You like him, don't you?"

Cough.

I was so startled that I choked. I hadn't expected her to be so direct.

Trying to calm down, I cleared my throat. "What are you talking about?" It wasn't a pleasant experience to hear someone else talk about feelings that I wasn't even willing to admit to myself. I desperately avoided her gaze. "I simply left them lying around because I didn't feel like reading them."

"Don't lie to me. What kind of person refuses to read her fiancé's letters? Something happened between you two, didn't it?" she asked sharply, and I stared out the window without responding.

Lies had been my tactic so far, but there was no knowing when my tongue would betray me. It was better to stay silent. I prayed the carriage would hurry up as I looked out the window.

"Mary, are you even listening to me?" Aria said, her voice growing louder.

Soon enough, I noticed very familiar scenery outside.

"We're here, my la—"

Clunk.

Before the horseman could finish, I dashed out the door.

"Mary!"

Ignoring Aria's voice, I ran into the mansion. I returned to my room, the newspapers still in my hand, and sighed as I put them on my desk again. To one side were the scattered letters I hadn't been able to organize yet.

With another deep sigh, I gazed down at the sealed envelopes. I wasn't sure if I had any right to read them now or reply to them. It was clear that I couldn't avoid doing so forever, and I did appreciate Ethen's feelings for me.

But even without my sense of duty toward Aria, I had some fatal flaws.

As if it wasn't worrying enough that I'd been pushing him away all this time, I didn't have the ability to tell him how I felt. I would be lucky if I didn't blurt out something atrocious like: "If you like me that much, it looks like I have no choice. I'll let you date me."

To be honest, in my current state, I probably wasn't capable of forming a proper relationship with anyone, let alone Ethen. I wanted him to think well of me, and I didn't want to be saying such stupid, disrespectful things in his presence all the time.

"Mary!"

I was sitting in front of my desk, thinking, when Aria burst through the door without knocking.

"What? You didn't even knock!" I said angrily, caught off guard.

"Oh, I'm sorry." Aria looked put out, but that didn't last long. She remembered why she'd come and looked at me, her face serious. "I noticed something seemed off between you two at the duchess' party. Something *is* going on, isn't it?"

"It's none of your business. Please leave me alone," I said, my words sharper than usual because I was frustrated by her questioning.

She made a sad puppy face. "You don't want to talk to me?"

"No, it's not that..." I wondered if I should comfort her or reiterate what I had said so that she would leave me alone.

"I'm sorry. I thought we were close enough to talk about this sort of thing," Aria said glumly.

I felt a prick in my conscience. *Oh, what the hell.* I closed my eyes.

"I don't know what to say... How am I supposed to write him back?"

"You should still read them, at least. Imagine how desperate he must be to get an answer from you."

Just yesterday, I'd been the one eager to get Aria together with Edville. But the tables had turned, leaving me sorely puzzled. *I had a good reason to do that, but why is Aria so eager to improve my relationship with Ethen?*

"You know, it's almost like you're a close friend of Lord Ethen. Why are you so interested?"

"Please don't think such a thing!" Aria said with a wave of her hand. "I have no interest in Lord Ethen."

"Then why do you keep talking about him?"

"Of course it's not because I'm interested in him. It's you I'm thinking about." Aria said, sounding flabbergasted.

I blinked and stared at her. "You're thinking about me?"

I had tried my best to avoid thinking about Ethen, and I'd almost never talked about him because I didn't want her to notice that I was concerned about him. *How is Aria so certain that she is doing what is best for me?*

"You like him," she said again, and I blushed, unable to even cough this time.

"As I said, how are you so sure?"

Aria blinked at me slowly, as if she didn't understand the question. "How do you expect me not to know?"

We slowly blinked while looking at each other, both of us unable to understand the other. It was Aria who broke the awkward silence.

"I'm surprised that you thought that I wouldn't know. You know, your emotions are quite obvious, more often than not…"

I looked back on my own behavior. *Am I that obvious?* I don't look into a mirror while I speak, so I wasn't sure, but maybe she was right.

"How could you know what I'm thinking just by looking at my face? You're mistaken."

"Even now, your face tells me I've hit the nail on the head."

I felt myself flinch. I should have maintained a shameless front. Feeling some belated regret, I sighed.

"I'm just busy, that's all…"

"I'll be busy rehearsing with the troupe members from now on, and you'll have more time on your hands. So read them," she said, clapping her hands together with a smile. Her eyes glowed, as if threatening that she would launch into a barrage of questions if I didn't reach for a letter right away. I picked one up with a trembling hand.

"This is no big deal."

This was nothing. They were just letters. I was sure they didn't contain anything noteworthy. Ethen wasn't standing in front of me, and I didn't have to read the letters out loud. *I can simply pretend to read them.*

Telling myself such things, I raised the envelope to eye level. They were nothing but a few scraps of paper. However, the envelope felt much heavier than usual.

"Mary, you should remove the seal first," Aria said, handing me a paper knife. I was so nervous that I'd been about to tear open the envelope.

With a deep breath, I removed the seal. When I slowly took out the letter within, Ethen's flowing script greeted my eyes. The paper seemed to be rippling, almost as if it was happy to finally see the light after a few days.

"Mary, are you all right?" Aria asked worriedly. Apparently, I'd been standing very awkwardly as I tried to move my eyes over to the letters.

I nodded, pretending to be fine. "This is nothing. It's just a letter," I claimed. But I couldn't quite bring myself to read it.

Aria finally decided she had pushed me far enough. "Mary, you don't have to read it if you don't want to."

"What are you saying? I feel fine."

"I just wanted to know why you weren't reading them and what happened between you two. I didn't mean that you should force yourself. I'm sorry."

I lowered the letter. "It's nothing much. This is nothing..."

"No. You don't have to tell me anything if you don't want to."

I'm more worried about what you'll think if I don't say anything now. Well, it doesn't matter anymore. Things have gotten as bad as they possibly could already.

"I've been too busy, is all. Really. Why do you think I'm lying? Why would I lie to you about this?" I shouted, continuing the lies that I knew she could see through.

"It's just..."

It's never going to work out anyway. I didn't want either of us—me or Ethen—to hope. Our relationship wasn't the sort that could be repaired by fixing one problem. It was a coiled-up mess, and I couldn't figure out where to even begin.

"It's no big deal," I said, turning away, unable to finish my sentence. "It's as you said, Aria. You said your happiness doesn't come from love. I'm the same way." I didn't know where my happiness lay or what I wanted, but I nonchalantly continued. "That's all there is to it."

I stared at the desk. The folded letter was sitting on top of it, its contents as hidden as they had been before I'd opened it.

"Mary," Aria said. "I didn't know where to find my happiness from the start." She didn't mention the letters or Ethen. "I know I sounded like a know-it-all, but I hardly know anything. I'm not strong enough to overcome every hardship on my own, either. However..." She took my empty hand in hers. "Just like you taught me where my happiness lies, I want to do the same for you."

CHAPTER ONE HUNDRED AND TWENTY-EIGHT

Where my happiness lies? I thought, a stunned look on my face.

"I'm already quite happy. I told you I would make you the greatest prima donna in the empire. That plan is going well, so why wouldn't I be happy?"

Although I may have felt uncomfortable, it didn't mean I was unhappy. Despite my plan not being thoroughly thought out, I was making significant progress towards accomplishing it.

"I know that," she said, nodding. "But happiness doesn't come from just one thing." She squeezed my hands harder as she looked at the letters I'd left on my desk. "I want you to be able to enjoy all sorts of things. I feel sorry because I feel like I've taken too much away from your own life because of my frustrating behavior."

"Why would you think that?" I asked, shaking my head firmly. "You don't need to feel that way. I am not upset with you. Indeed, the fact that you would think that about me hurts me more."

"I feel the same way." Aria looked at me. "You probably don't realize it, but you're always looking at Lord Ethen when you're with him."

"It's because he's handsome." Nobody could deny that. His face was one that attracted attention. I tried to be dismissive about it. "It's not because of some special reason."

"And though you seem uncomfortable when you're with him, it feels to me like you just don't know how to act around him."

I gulped. She'd hit the nail on the head. It was true that I didn't know how to act around him. That was my biggest problem.

"You seem different than usual when you're around him. And when I see that side of you, you know what I always think?" Aria smiled. "You two are far too careful around each other, but that just makes you an even more charming couple."

I felt a sting in my heart as she smiled at me. I knew we weren't real lovers or anything.

"I don't know what it is you're so afraid of, but he likes you too, and you're already engaged. You'll be family one day, and you're bound to feel more natural around each other."

Will that really happen? I wondered, staring at her.

"And when I imagine that future, I know it'll make you happy."

Aria was saying she believed I'd be happy with Ethen, but I was afraid. I had a poor reputation, and I wasn't really good at anything besides what I was doing with Aria now. I was just a marquess' daughter with a disastrous tongue.

Can I really be happy with Ethen? I would be lucky if I didn't inconvenience him in some way.

"Mary, you're never cowardly with anything, but you're very fearful when it comes to him," she said, unaware of my feelings. "That only drew my attention more because it told me how much you liked him."

Is this the way other people see me when I'm with him? I pouted, waiting for her to continue.

"It might seem silly for me to say this to you, but... don't be too afraid. You're a good person. Just like you made me happy, I want you to be loved and be happy."

"Of course. Who do you think I am?" My tongue was boasting again, despite my complete lack of confidence inside. I wondered where this endless self-affection came from. I hadn't been able to lie about anything else, even if I wasn't too knowledgeable about it.

"That's right. That's the sort of person you are," Aria said, beaming and nodding at me. "So don't be afraid. You're free to make any choice you like, so I want you to decide with only yourself and what you want in mind."

I didn't really know what that was, but I was sure of one thing.

Can I really do that?

Aria's words were giving me hope, though I knew I shouldn't be hopeful. This meant I, too, hadn't been able to give up on Ethen completely.

After Aria left my room, I took a deep breath and sat down in front of my desk. I wasn't sure what would happen, but I couldn't run away forever. I figured the first thing I should do was read the letters. I picked up the envelope I'd opened earlier and started to read.

The first letter was quite ordinary.

The weather was very nice today. The garden looked even more refreshing than usual, reminding me of the tea we had last time. My chef is looking forward to showing off his skills the next time you visit.

I wonder if I may be allowed to hope that you will visit the mansion again one of these sunny days?

—Ethen Frangert

The tea we'd had in the duke's garden was when I'd told Ethen I wanted to call off the engagement. It seemed very much like Ethen to mention that day as if he had completely forgotten about that.

I opened the next letter.

My father told me that you have been preparing a special project in collaboration with the imperial family. You are always hardworking, and I do not doubt the results will be fantastic.

Since you enjoy what you are doing, it makes me want to wish the best results for you even more.

Please do not overwork yourself and have fun.

—Ethen Frangert

Each letter was about common, everyday things, but they revealed his affection for me every time. I could see the way he wanted to express his feelings for me without making me uncomfortable, and the whole time I read them, I felt a tickling sensation in my heart.

I continued to read his letters for some time. I'd been avoiding them for so long, but now that I'd started reading them, I couldn't hold back.

I am worried that you might have been upset after the incident at the party yesterday. Did you get home safely?

I am sorry that I did not recognize what was going on sooner or be of much help to you. While I cannot officially find fault with the House of Mirvaseba over what happened, my mother will be delivering a firm warning to the countess. I hope you aren't too upset about her meaningless comments.

I wish I could help you somehow and am sorry I cannot seem to do much. Perhaps it is my greed speaking when I say I want to be someone close enough to be by your side and help you. I may not be good enough for such a role, but I will do my best to be worthy of you.

I pray you will answer these silly letters one of these days.

—Ethen Frangert

This letter, which had arrived after the duchess' party, was longer than the others. Not only that, but based on the ink marks, I could also see traces of hesitation throughout, as if he had given a lot of thought to the contents. I wondered what he had been thinking as he wrote. Even though I was the one who'd refused his attention and help, his letter was full of self-reproach.

Sniff... Tears welled up in my eyes for some reason. I stared at the letter for some time.

I was the one who wasn't good enough, the one who had a fatal flaw that made me fear I would do him more harm than good.

Is this what he had been thinking while I avoided him, trying to hide my faults? Perhaps everything I tried to do for his sake would only end up hurting both of us.

The tears refused to stop.

I wished I were a normal person without this damned tongue that always made trouble. Of all the mysterious things that had happened to me, my troublesome tongue seemed to be the worst curse. But I couldn't come clean to others about my story, either. My tongue wouldn't allow it, but even if I were to tell someone, nothing would change. In fact, things might only get worse.

If I told people that I wasn't the real Mary Bell, but a reader of the novel this world was based on, and I'd been transported into her body... I'd be lucky if people didn't call me crazy and ostracize me.

Perhaps even Ethen, who seemed so desperate to win my love now, would turn against me. I imagined the shock that would fill his face, and it made me shudder. It might be better never to see him again than to have to see such a look on his face. I wiped the tears from my eyes.

Is leaving Ethen in this state the best I can do? Do I have to give up on him, without even trying to do anything?

I shook my head. There was nothing I could do, no matter how much thinking I did.

At least I can help Aria achieve her newfound happiness. I should probably be happy with that. Even in this horrible body, I can at least do that. I decided to think on the bright side, trying to calm down.

Aria had told me to reach for my own happiness, but I had no idea where it lay or how to achieve it. The only thing I could do now was barely read through the letters containing Ethen's worries and fears.

I picked up another letter from my desk. My eyes were so full of tears that I couldn't even make out the seal on the envelope. I ripped it open, thinking all the envelopes were from Ethen anyway.

But contrary to my expectations, the letter wasn't from Ethen.

I wiped the tears from my eyes as I took in the very short but powerful message within.

I know that you are no ordinary person.

This mysterious message wasn't one I could easily ignore.

CHAPTER
ONE HUNDRED
AND TWENTY-NINE

The very first sentence of the letter was enough to grab my attention.

I know that you are no ordinary person.

I reread it several times, unable to figure out why this man had written such a thing to me.

—Vante Luce

The seal that I hadn't been able to see because of my tears belonged to the House of Luce. I remembered getting a letter not long after the hunting competition. I had put it aside, not thinking it was worth reading, and it had probably gotten mixed in with Ethen's letters as I piled them up.

While I could guess how the letter had gotten here, I had no clue why he'd written such a letter to me. Our very first meeting was strange, to be certain. He had spoken to me as if he knew me, although we'd never exchanged a word before. Then he'd vanished as if disappointed. At the hunting competition, he'd come up to me again with that annoying look on his face.

Most people would have burned this letter without a second thought, but I couldn't dismiss it so easily.

If you want to know how I know this about you, go and collect the letter I left with an employee at the Lebonae Bakery. I will be waiting.

The letter was brusque and short, and after reading it so many times that I could have quoted it from memory, I fell into a dilemma. While his claim sounded silly, there was something about it I couldn't quite ignore.

Though the real Vante Luce did not seem quite the same as the one in the novel, as a rule, characters were not completely different from the way they'd been portrayed. Though he acted strangely around me, he'd had a good reputation before that, just like in the novel. Even the rumor that he could seemingly see right through people had been right.

"I can't ignore this outright…"

It bothered me too much. I tapped at the name "Lebonae Bakery" and started to think.

I was so unnerved by the letter that I forgot to cry, and I glowered at it for a while.

"I need to go out for a short while. Help me get ready."

"Yes, my lady. What dress would you like to wear?" Annie said, bowing.

"The plainest one you can find."

"The plainest one… my lady?" Annie looked at me quizzically. It made sense because Mary's wardrobe had no plain dresses at all—she abhorred anything that wasn't fancy.

"Yes. I need to stay out of sight."

"Yes, my lady," Annie said, bowing with a grave look on her face. It was a difficult order.

The letter was almost a month old now. I couldn't be sure that the letter Vante had presumably left at the bakery was still there. Even so, I had to find out if he really knew something about me and, if so, how.

What if… he knows why all of this absurdity happened in the first place?

I had to find out.

I couldn't be gone for long because, as far as the public knew, Ethen and I were still engaged. If it became known that I'd met with Vante, someone who had openly flirted with me, in private, it would do neither Ethen nor me any good. It was best that I return without being seen. As it happened, Aria was starting her rehearsals with the rest of the troupe, so I could leave without her knowledge.

"My lady, these are the plainest dresses I could find." Annie came in solemnly while I was lost in thought and showed me a few dresses. I could see that she had tried, but they were still too showy for my liking.

"You think these are plain?" *I understand you put in some effort, but this isn't good enough...*

Annie's face scrunched up, her eyes tearing up at my reaction. I had a feeling this outing was going to be anything but easy.

"My lady, are you sure you want to go alone? You should at least take Lilian with you."

"I've told you enough times that I'll be fine. I'm not a child."

"Even so..." Annie sounded worried. While I was grateful for her concern, I couldn't take anyone with me today—not even the trusty Lilian. This visit had to do with my most important secret, and I had to be extremely cautious.

"Anyway, this won't take long. Don't tell anyone I went out, and just go about your business, all right? You're the only person I've talked to about this trip."

"Only me?" Annie seemed strangely moved as she pointed at herself. She smiled, apparently pleased that this was to be our little secret. "Of course. I won't tell anyone. Please don't worry, my lady."

When did she start trusting me like this? It didn't seem so long ago when she had apologized profusely at every turn.

I gave her a pleasant look. "Yes, you go about your business. I'm leaving." I closed the carriage door as I waved at her.

"The Lebonae Bakery, my lady?" the horseman said.

"Yes. You know where it is, right?"

"Of course," he replied, giving a bow visible through the carriage window. "It's just that... it's not a place where nobles are known to frequent. It's not very popular even among the commoners. I wouldn't have known about it, either, if it wasn't near where I live," he said cautiously.

I didn't care if the Lebonae Bakery was a tiny establishment in a seedy building or some huge, well-to-do shop downtown. As a matter of fact, maybe I preferred the former. That way, I wouldn't have to worry about people seeing me.

"What business is it of yours?" *I'm sorry, but I can't tell you the details.*

The horseman gasped and clammed up, which was clearly what I was telling him to do.

"Get moving."

"Yes, of course, my lady." The horseman shut the window and scurried toward his seat.

I'd grown very displeased with him because of the last time he'd been tasked with driving Aria, and he'd been trying very hard to recover my favor since then. In truth, I knew there was no way to stop Aria if she really wanted to leave. I no longer blamed the hapless horseman, but I decided to take advantage of the situation while it lasted.

"Here we go, then," he said.

The carriage moved away from the mansion, and before long I arrived at the Lebonae Bakery.

"Is this really the place?" I doubted my eyes for a moment when I saw the shoddy sign. I'd expected a moderately respectable establishment, since the son of a count had left his letter here, but this shop was all but falling apart.

"I thought you knew, my lady?" the horseman said in confusion.

"There are no other Lebonae Bakeries anywhere?"

"Of course not. Not as far as I know. Lebonae Bakery? Who would give their bakery such a simple name but the old Lady Lebonae—Ahh!"

The horseman's words were cut off with a scream. A cane had landed on his head, hitting bone with a loud, ringing thwack.

"You've got a problem with the name of my bakery?"

"Oh God! I'm sorry! Stop hitting me."

The staff that had rapped the man on the head two more times stopped only after the apology.

"Grandmother, you shouldn't go around hitting people like that," said a woman, rushing out of the shop with a troubled look on her face and pulling the old woman back.

"He called the name of my bakery simple. So, I gave him a simple reaction, that's all."

"Oh, my goodness. Grandmother! I told you to ignore comments like that. What's wrong with 'Lebonae Bakery'? It's a very pretty name, no matter what people might say." The woman, having settled the old woman down, apologized to the horseman. "I'm sorry. She can be a little... Oh, Mr. Hans?" The woman's eyes widened when she recognized the horseman. "What are you doing here? You said you never wanted to taste my grandmother's bread again... Whoops!"

"What's that?" The old woman looked daggers at the horseman again.

The man backed away slowly, afraid of getting another blow to the head. "No, that's not what I meant. My wife has learned to bake, you see, and I no longer need to buy bread..."

"And I don't want customers like you anyway, you moron." The old woman waved her staff and clicked her tongue.

What is going on here? I was watching them, uncertain how to react, when the young woman spoke to me. She was presumably an employee at the bakery.

"You look like a noblewoman. What are you doing at a place like this?"

Hans seemed to know them well, so she probably knew that I was the daughter of Hans' employer. I cleared my throat at her politely worded question.

"Is this really Lebonae Bakery?"

Even though this was a run-down place, I'd thought I might find some secret messaging channel since Vante had left his letter here. But this was just an ordinary bakery. I was still suspicious, and she seemed puzzled by the question.

"Yes, this is it."

Hmm. Perhaps nobody would suspect that an important letter would be kept here, and Vante had put it here for that reason. Doing my best to understand the situation, I nodded to her.

"You must be the woman. I can tell," said the old woman vigorously. She was pointing her staff at me now.

The young woman gasped. "Grandmother! I'm sorry, my lady. Old age has affected her memory, you see…"

"Don't you dare insinuate that I'm senile. I'm perfectly fine," the old woman grumbled. "Anyway, this is the bakery you've been looking for. Please come inside. It's not something we can talk about on the street, don't you think?" The old woman's voice was too clear and ringing to belong to someone suffering from dementia.

It seemed pretty certain that she knew something about me, so I decided to listen to what she had to say. With a dubious look, I nodded my head.

CHAPTER ONE HUNDRED AND THIRTY

"Grandmother…"

"Ey! I told you to leave me be."

The young woman, looking worried, hovered around the table where the old woman and I sat, but the old woman seemed annoyed by this.

"Got plenty of time on your hands, have you? Have you completed our order forms?"

"Oh!" said the woman, her eyes widening. "I'd forgotten about that."

"Tsk. You're in no position to worry about me. You puzzle me sometimes."

The old woman, having chased the younger woman away, turned her deep, unreadable eyes to me. She seemed different from when she had socked the horseman over the head or complained to the woman who seemed to be her granddaughter.

Slowly, I opened my mouth. "If you know who I am, then you must have the letter."

"It's not only the letter I have. I know a lot of things," she said with a chuckle. The laugh gave me the creeps, and I decided to get out of here as quickly as possible.

"Then bring me that letter already. I'm a busy woman. I don't have time to waste."

"Perhaps it's my age… I can't quite remember if I used it as a fire starter or for picking up some garbage, my lady."

What? So, you don't have the letter?

Outraged, I shot to my feet. "Are you kidding me?" I shouted.

"Grandmother!" The young woman, jumping with fright, rushed over and threw her arms around the old woman. She bowed her head toward me. "I don't know what she has said to anger you but let me apologize for her. She is so old… She isn't always in her right mind. Please forgive her. I beg of you, my lady."

"Yvette, this isn't necessary. You go about your business."

"Grandmother, this is no time to be obstinate," said Yvette, looking frustrated.

The old woman turned to me again, not looking flustered in the least. "The things I know will be of more use to you than the letter. I only got rid of it because it was unnecessary."

"And how am I supposed to believe that?" I asked, glaring at her with my arms crossed. *Why did Vante leave the letter here with this old woman?* A scowl appeared on my face as I thought about Vante's actions, none of which made sense. "I don't like the person who left the letter here, nor the person he left it with," I said sharply.

Yvette fell to her knees. "My lady, please have mercy on us."

But I couldn't take out my anger on an innocent girl. I brusquely said to her, "Get up. People will think I threw a tantrum in here."

"T-that's not true," she said, shooting to her feet like a spring.

"Yes, Yvette. You don't need to do this."

"Grandmother, that's enough."

If the letter wasn't here, there was no reason for me to stay. I wondered if I should get in touch with Vante. *I don't like that idea...*

Frowning, I got up from the chair. "Forget it. It'll be a waste of my time to get angry with the likes of you. I don't have that much free time on my hands."

I should just leave. That's what I was thinking as I got up, when Yvette bowed to me repeatedly in gratitude.

"Thank you. Thank you, my lady."

"My lady," the old woman said, apparently not at all bothered by Yvette's urgent apologies. "If you must leave after hearing what I'm about to tell you, I won't stop you."

"Go on and say it, then," I said, mesmerized by the deep, clear eyes that couldn't be those of an old woman suffering from dementia. I was going to leave anyway, but I had nothing to lose by waiting for her to say one more thing.

Her next words made me stiffen with shock.

"It's a very uncomfortable thing, isn't it, to be unable to speak the way you want?"

I looked down at the old woman, dumbfounded. Yvette blinked, not understanding the situation, but we stared at each other for some time in silence.

"Why don't you sit back down? This will be a lengthy conversation," the old woman said, breaking the silence.

I sat down as instructed, unable to say anything.

"Yvette, go bring some tea."

"Yes. What kind?" Yvette said, looking up.

"My favorite."

"We're out of that tea, and I'll have to go out to buy some... Ugh, fine."

Having sent Yvette away with ease, the old woman gave a smile of satisfaction. "Now we can finally talk comfortably."

"Who are you?" I asked.

"What do you mean? I'm an old woman. There's nothing special about me at all."

How could an ordinary old woman recognize my state the moment she saw me?

I frowned at her. "Stop joking around and get to the point."

Magic existed in the novel, but its use was not widespread. There was almost no mention of it at all except for magic stones, and from what I had learned from living in this world, magic was all but forgotten. It was featured in old stories, and some relics of it remained, but nobody used it anymore.

"Haha."

So how does this woman know about me? I took a deep breath. "Enough of this. Get down to business. If you know everything, are you trying to toy with me? Why do you keep changing the subject?"

"I'm an old woman who has nothing to do, my lady. I need a companion to talk to." Unlike me, she still seemed relaxed. I would have liked nothing better than to threaten her into telling me everything she knew, but I had no choice but to let her have her way. I was the one who needed the information.

"What will I get in return for being a companion?"

"I'll tell you something only I know about."

Something only she knows about? My ears pricked up. "How long will this take?"

"Hmm... I don't know about that. That depends on what you tell me," said the old lady, with a grin on her face. "Now that I'm old, nothing interests me more than young people's stories."

Now I was beginning to wonder how Vante had discovered this woman and what she'd told him to give him the confidence to write me that letter.

"It's a trifling wish from an old woman. Please understand."

I could tell she was anything but an ordinary old woman. *How did Vante get information from her?* I wished I could go see him right away and ask.

"What kind of story do you want to hear?"

"Hmm. I think anything you tell me will be interesting... but I do enjoy the romantic ones the most."

She wants me to tell her a romantic story? I've never even dated someone before, so how am I supposed to do that?

"Anything else?"

"Anything goes. You have much to talk about, don't you? Things you've never been able to tell anyone. Any of that will serve just fine," she said, as if she knew everything. "Then perhaps I could tell you how to get what you want most."

What I wanted most was to be freed from this damned tongue. *Is she offering to provide a solution to this?*

I shot to my feet. "Do you mean that?"

"I assure you that it is not a losing trade for you," she said, smiling.

"What are you?"

"Just an old woman."

A normal old woman wouldn't know these things. I stared at her with resentment, and the woman chuckled.

"You seem nervous, so let me tell you one little thing," she said, as if she was being generous. I sat back down and waited for her next words.

"They say magic is gone from this world, but that's only what the ignorant ones think. The visible effects of magic may have vanished, but some people are still born with it."

"And you're one of them?"

She shrugged and grinned. "I can't do anything fancy. I just see things that others don't notice. For example..." She stared at my face—or rather, right at my lips. "I can tell that your soul doesn't belong in this world, but only one part of your body retains the vestiges of the old one."

I stared at her in astonishment. "The vestiges of the old soul? What does that mean?"

"You go first if you want me to tell you more," she said, shaking her head. "The young man I met last time told me a lot of interesting things as well."

"Are you talking about Lord Vante?"

The old woman laughed. *Of course it's him. He's the one who told me about this place.* I was curious about what he had told her, but this old woman probably wouldn't tell me anything without me first giving her something.

I have to say something. Where should I begin?

"Is it difficult to decide?"

"Yes. This is rather sudden. I can't just tell you the story of my life from beginning to end," I said, my brusque tongue taking over.

The old woman seemed understanding of my secret, however, instead of being offended. "Of course. Maybe I should ask some questions, then?"

"If you want." *That does seem like the easier option.* I nodded and looked at her.

"In that case... Hmm—"

"Wait, one moment." An urgent voice cut the old woman off. A man had come in, doubled over as he tried to catch his breath. "Nice to see you again, Lady Mary."

I couldn't speak.

Vante took a deep breath as he looked up at me.

CHAPTER
ONE HUNDRED
AND THIRTY-ONE

Judging from the sweat on Vante's forehead, he seemed to have run here in a hurry.

"Madam, I told you to contact me."

"Unlike you, I don't have personal attendants. How could I have told you so quickly?" the old woman grumbled, shaking her head. "And why does it matter? You came here on time just fine."

"Forget it. I wasn't expecting much, anyway," Vante said with a sigh. "As you said, that's not what's important." He turned to me as he said those words, but I avoided his gaze.

"Right. In any case, since we've met again like this, I suppose there is some talking that needs to be done."

There was no way to avoid speaking with him. This was an opportunity to handle everything at once. I tried to look on the bright side as I said, "You wrote something absurd in your letter, saying I was not an ordinary person. You must have known something when you wrote that nonsense."

"I learned of it by coincidence. I have a feeling that you will not think of this conversation as a waste of time by the time we are done," Vante said with a distasteful smile. "It wouldn't be thoughtful of me if I did not share what I know about you. If I tell you a secret first, perhaps you'll be able to believe me more easily."

Vante's secret? I wondered what it was. Interested, I relaxed my guard a little and looked at him. "So, you have a secret?"

"Yes, just like you... or perhaps not as much as you, but I also have a secret I do not share with others," he said with a smile. "Other people wouldn't believe me if I told them, but I think you would."

I wondered why he was being so pompous. With a gulp, I waited for him to continue.

"I can see people's colors."

That took a moment for me to process. *See people's colors? What does that even mean?*

"The colors represent their true selves... so to speak. I can see their character in color. People say I have great discernment. But it is only partly true."

I eyed him suspiciously, understanding what he meant. "What makes you so sure I'll believe you?"

"I have never once doubted these eyes." His completely unrelated answer confused me.

"Why is that relevant?"

"Well, I actually doubted them for the first time recently."

What is this, a confession? I didn't know why he was telling me this. I felt disgruntled, but his next words allowed me to understand.

"Your color... it changed."

If he could see people's characters in color, then my color would not have been the same as Mary's. While I had been no saint, at least I hadn't been as terrible a person as Mary had been in the novel.

"That was why I was interested in you. You used to have a color so red I could make it out from a distance."

Red was a warning color, and it suited the original Mary Bell very well. I somehow found myself understanding perfectly and nodded as I listened.

"But at the birthday celebration, your color was suddenly green. It was the opposite color, and generally a safe one as well."

A safe color? I looked at him questioningly.

"The colors indicate people's character," he added. "They help me judge whether it is safe to approach a person or not."

This explanation cleared things up completely, so I nodded again.

"But unlike the color, which had changed, you seemed to exhibit no changes in your behavior. No—it would be more precise to say your behavior did change somewhat, but not the way you spoke or looked."

That's because I can't control my tongue and facial expressions.

"That was why I doubted my eyes for the very first time. I'd always taken my ability for granted, but that result puzzled me sorely."

I now knew why Vante had acted the way he did. Being a person who was literally not of this world, I didn't find it surprising that he had been confused—though, to be honest, I was the biggest victim in all of this. I'd read the novel, and thoroughly at that, but nowhere had it said that Vante had this sort of hidden ability.

"Aria seemed to glow with a white light. It dazzled him and took his breath away, causing him to doubt his eyes for a moment."

Wait, was that part sort of a hint? But who would think that to be a reference to a mystical ability and not just a stereotypical description of the female lead?

"So, did you do a background check on me after that?"

"No, of course not," Vante said, shaking his hands in denial. "I began looking more deeply into my own ability, rather than you. No matter how much I searched through the records of my ancestors, nobody had experienced what I had."

Of course. It can't be common for someone to enter this novel's world like I did. I nodded slightly.

"The ability runs in the family, so I met various people and searched through the records, trying hard to find out more about it. Then I met Madam Lebonae here," he said, glancing at the old woman.

She looked ordinary enough. *What secret is she hiding?*

"Was there something special about her?" I asked cautiously.

"Yes, though I think I would have dismissed what I saw if I hadn't seen you first," he said with a smile.

"What did you notice?" I asked out of curiosity.

Vante answered, "She had no color."

"Well, you just told her everything about me. There goes my chance to hear something interesting," the woman huffed at him. "You can't be stealing the fun from under people's noses like this."

"You're hiding much more than this. Don't try to fool me," Vante said nonchalantly. "The moment she saw me, she recognized my ability and what family I was from. I believed she could provide the answer to my questions."

This was hard to believe, but so was my story. "All right. But why bother to tell me about it?" There was a question I still hadn't found the answer to. Vante must have received all the answers he needed after meeting this elderly woman. *So why did he want to see me?* I looked at him, still a bit suspicious.

"She was interested in you, and if what she told me was true, I believed you'd also need help."

He wanted to help me? I looked at him, touched. I'd never said a kind thing to him before. *You're a good person, aren't you?*

"And I also wanted to confirm that there was nothing wrong with my ability."

This seemed to be the main reason, but I decided to ignore it. Clearing my throat, I said, "I understand. I thought you were out of your mind, but I'm relieved that it wasn't the case." Now that the misunderstanding was cleared up and my guard had come down a little, I felt less tense.

"I wanted to make sure. And Madam Lebonae was confident that a meeting with her would be of help to you," Vante said.

"Of course. I never lie," she said proudly.

I didn't know what she was exactly, but as suspected, she wasn't an ordinary person.

"This tactless young man has told you everything there is to know about me, but I know a few things that might help you, young lady." She turned to me with a serious look. "So, what'll it be?"

I flinched at her gaze, but the answer was obvious. *How many people like this old woman exist in this world?* There might not be another chance for me to meet someone who understood my position. The old lady apparently knew how to achieve my biggest goal, and I had nothing to lose by telling her a little of my story if I could glean that knowledge from her.

"I'll answer whatever question you might have for me. But be aware, you'll have to answer my questions, too—"

"I may joke around at times, but I do not lie. Don't worry," the old woman said conversationally, trying to set my mind at ease.

"In that case..." *Where do I begin?* I took a deep breath and opened my mouth.

"Oh dear. The tea shops that sell Flora leaves are all closed today..." At that moment, Yvette came in, talking tactlessly. That forced me to shut up.

I had no idea why people had to interrupt every time I had something important to say. It seemed pretty clear that the God of Timing, if there was one, hated me. Grumbling inside, I looked at Yvette.

"The trip took way too long. You should have just drunk what we have in the shop."

"But that was the only tea I wanted. You should have bought some in advance," the old woman said, not looking at all nervous about the conversation being interrupted like I was.

"Oh, goodness me! I forgot to ask what kind of tea you prefer, my lady."

I was in no mood for a casual teatime. I waved my hand in the air. "Any tea is fine."

"Give her the same tea as mine. It's excellent for your health," the old woman said.

I was not interested in tea. Pursing my lips, I watched Yvette walk away. She seemed to know nothing. *Is it all right to continue our conversation in her presence?*

"We have plenty of time. No need to hurry, my lady," the old woman said casually, as if she'd read my mind. "We'll have other days to talk."

"But I *am* in a hurry. I need to do this as quickly as—" I needed my tongue to function normally again for me to speak with Ethen. There were less than two weeks left until the deadline.

"Yvette will be cleaning the warehouse at eleven tomorrow morning. I will be alone in the shop," she said, her calmness contrasting sharply with my growing anxiety.

CHAPTER ONE HUNDRED AND THIRTY-TWO

In the end, I had to return to the mansion without getting a clear answer. I would be able to hear the rest tomorrow morning, but that didn't ease my frustration.

I let out a sigh. It was difficult not to feel impatient after learning about the possibility of being freed from my terrible tongue. Perhaps I wouldn't have felt this way if I still believed nothing would ever change.

Biting my fingernails, I lapsed into thought. Never once had I believed that my situation would improve. It had been impossible for me to know why my tongue refused to do my bidding, so I hadn't had a clue how to fix it. But now that I had been told it could be fixed, I couldn't help but consider the possibilities.

If my tongue returned to normal and I could finally say the things I wanted the way I wanted to say them...

If, at the very least, I could avoid being so much trouble to the people who mattered to me...

There is nothing more I could wish for. For the first time in a while, I actually felt hopeful as I waited.

If it ever happened, I would first work on recovering the relationships my brilliant mouth had ruined, starting with the rude way I'd spoken to Anna and Annie. I would be able to give proper compliments to Aria as well. Not only that, I would fight less often with May, who was always complaining but in truth wanted what was best for me.

Most importantly of all, perhaps I could finally speak properly of my feelings to the person I wanted to speak to the most.

When my thoughts reached that point, I blushed and hung my head, blinking silently.

I wondered if I was getting ahead of myself when nothing was certain, but a person could dream. I had every right to imagine things, at the very least. It was with this excuse that I nodded to myself.

"Mary."

"Whoa!"

I was standing out on the balcony, lost in thought, and feeling the wind, when Aria returned all of a sudden and called me. She was dressed for going out and holding some sheet music in her hand.

"What are you doing, leaning dangerously on the balustrade like that?"

"Just getting some air," I said, running my hand through my hair in embarrassment. "How was rehearsal? Nobody was mean to you, right?"

"Hahaha..." She laughed awkwardly instead of denying it.

So, there was someone like that. I narrowed my eyes after easily recognizing what her laugh had meant. "What happened?"

"It was nothing. It was my first day, you know. I can't expect everything to go well on the first day. I'm sure we'll get to know each other better soon enough—"

"No, that's not what I asked. What happened?"

She said nothing. She was probably nervous that I would do something to the people who were mean to her if she told me.

"You don't think I can find out if you refuse to tell me?"

Just because she wouldn't tell me didn't mean I didn't have other ways of finding out. I knew where she'd been and what she'd been doing, so it would be an easy matter. I shrugged as I looked at her.

She seemed to know this as well. "Still, I am not going to tell you," she muttered slowly. "I told you I would take care of my own affairs."

"This is nothing. You shouldn't even consider it help."

"If I keep turning to you for every little thing, I won't be able to do anything on my own. Is that what you want?"

I stared at her with my mouth open. "That's not what I—"

"Anyway, I can't tell you. I'll take care of this myself. You have your own things to deal with." Aria glanced at my desk, which was littered with various opened letters. "I'm really fine. You don't need to worry about me," she said, backing away nervously as if afraid that I would demand she tell me again.

"Today was the first day I took part in a rehearsal under Baron Robert's direction. I was a bit worried, but he treated me like everyone else, which made things easier," she said, smoothly changing the subject.

That inflexible man seemed to know how to keep personal feelings out of his work, at least.

"Of course he should have done that," I said grumpily. "Considering the things he said to us, he can't be going around discriminating against you."

"And there were lots of nice people there, too. Some of them even knew me and said they'd heard my singing and liked it. I was delighted." Aria beamed. It seemed some of the members were kind toward her, just as some were not. She looked like she'd taken a load off her mind "Now that there's about a month and a half left until the performance, I'm going to do my best to make it a good one."

"Of course it will be. I'm the one who recognized your talent, remember?" Seeing the determination on her face, I thought better of my plan to punish everyone who'd been rude to her and engaged in a more peaceful conversation.

"Hahaha! You're right. Since it was you, of all people, I'm sure I'll be a great hit," Aria said with a big smile. "I'll do my best to give a great performance. I hope only good things happen to you until then, Mary."

Yeah, me, too. I hope I'll be free of my stupid tongue by that point.

With that thought, I nodded back at her.

I arrived at Lebonae Bakery the next day at eleven. *Is there really a way to get my mouth back to normal?* I took a deep breath in front of the door. I stood there for a while, unable to reach for the handle.

"Why are you standing out there like that?" The old woman, Madam Lebonae, opened the door for me. "Come in. I'm ready for guests," she said, guiding me inside. As she claimed, there was a table set with tea and a few cookies. "Yvette will be gone for at least an hour, so you don't need to worry that someone might interrupt. We open late and close late as well," she said, locking the door.

How can a bakery open late? I wondered, holding the teacup in front of me.

"Then let's pick up where we left off, shall we?"

I kept my eyes on her as I sipped. She looked perfectly ordinary. *How does she know people's secrets like this?*

"It's a very neat thing to see what others can't, but also quite inconvenient," she said. "If revealed, it's something that attracts people who would then be tempted to approach me and take advantage of me."

There seemed to be a lot of hidden meaning in her words, and I nodded. I was starting to realize she must have lived a very hard life.

"But now that I'm old and useless on the surface, life has gotten interesting." She chuckled. "The young man from the House of Luce? I recognized his power the moment I saw him. He might not know it, but I've seen his father—no, his grandfather. People like that are not easy to forget." She stared out into space, apparently thinking about Vante. "As magic faded from this world and my ability grew useless, I never thought I would see someone so interesting again. But what do you know? He came to see me first."

"Did you recognize me instantly as well?" I asked quickly.

She nodded. "I could imagine what to expect after he told me about you... but after I saw you in person, I realized I couldn't have failed to notice. Your wavelength is something I've never seen before in my entire life." She stared at me, looking at something that no one else could see, for quite a while. "You had an otherworldly wavelength... but the one near your mouth was definitely of this world. I knew right away that something interesting was afoot."

Something interesting? This is a terrible problem for me.

"You said you knew how to solve this problem?"

"I can't guarantee it will work... but yes, I think I do."

You can't guarantee it? My shoulders drooped in disappointment.

"But it's something I'm almost certain about," she added.

My disappointment remained, but I was too desperate not to give it a shot. I looked up again. "What do you suggest I do?"

"I can't tell you my prized secret so easily."

After hearing these words, I had to repress an urge to bang my fists on the table and yell, "That's not fair!"

"Tell me about you," she said. "I'd like to stave off my boredom, but I also need to know a few things about you if I'm to give you advice."

I calmed down a little and took a deep breath. "Fine. Where do I start?"

"Hmm... why don't you start with what matters to you the most?"

I'd anticipated her asking how I'd ended up in this world or how I managed to pass myself off as the original owner of this body, but this was a completely different question.

What matters to me the most? After a moment of thought, I said, "Me?" *Oh! Wait, that isn't what I wanted to say.* I cleared my throat and tried hard to say the right words.

"I'm the most important. And after that... there is the performance at the palace next month... and the people that are important to me."

If the performance went well, Aria would grow much closer to achieving her dream and happiness. That was what mattered the most. Then came the people that mattered to me in this world, such as Anna, Annie, Lilian, my parents, May, Ashley, and Maia. *And also...*

"Then there's my fiancé, Lord Ethen."

I spoke as confidently as I could, but there was no way I could keep from blushing. I finished my words with a bright red face.

ONE HUNDRED AND THIRTY-THREE

"I see. Then the solution I have for you just might work." Madam Lebonae gave a mysterious smile, but I didn't notice—because I was too busy trying not to look flustered.

This was probably the first time I'd admitted to thinking about him. That made me feel strange and shaken up inside.

"What is it?" I tried my best to act casually, though I could feel my face reddening.

"Haha! I'll tell you that after I've heard a bit more from you. It would be no fun if I told you already," she said with a teasing smile.

It wasn't difficult for me to tell her what she wanted, but this made me feel like I was being made fun of. I gave Madam Lebonae an angry look.

"Although I only recently learned of your secret, my lady, I've been hearing about you for quite some time," she said, sipping her tea. "Or to be more precise, about the lady that often accompanies you."

She was talking about Aria. I nodded. "I suppose you did. All commoners in the capital have probably heard about her at least once."

The way she'd influenced the festivals and how many performances had appeared thanks to her were indicators of her influence on the streets. It wasn't that surprising to hear that this old woman knew about her.

"I think it would be fun to hear about that, too," she said, chuckling.

About Aria? I wondered what to say. "There's nothing special to it. She had amazing talent, and I had the ability to make that talent shine."

"Hmm." Madam Lebonae's eyes widened a fraction, her interest in my story noticeably piqued.

"I was bored, with nothing else to do," I said, a hint of arrogance in my voice. "Who else could have brought Aria's voice to the streets? Haha. Nobody could have come up with such an idea."

"You must have enjoyed it very much," she said, watching me run a hand through my hair.

Enjoyed it? Of course I did. It had been the most joyful thing I'd ever done in this world. Without a hint of hesitation, I nodded. "Obviously. Why would I have done it if I didn't enjoy it?"

"Was the success something unexpected, then?"

"Of course it wasn't. How could I fail in anything I tried?"

She smiled again, noting my confidence.

"I knew we'd be successful."

"Was there anything that didn't go according to plan?"

I froze at her astute question. There had been things like that, too. To be honest, there had been a lot of them. I could think of multiple examples right off the bat.

"Yes, as with every endeavor."

My tongue was too proud to say what I wanted. Even if I knew where to begin, my tongue probably wouldn't have let me say it out loud. I stared at the woman, my lips moving but not making any sound. That brief silence, however, seemed to be enough to tell her about my condition.

"It doesn't look like I'll have any luck listening to a lengthy account. Let me tell you about myself, then." she said slowly, apparently realizing I wasn't able to say much. "You might not like being different from other people, but when I was younger, I was very proud that I was unique."

Being different from other people. I was like that in a lot of ways. And though it was a very useless difference that I couldn't control my tongue, I had also once taken pride in the fact that I was unique.

"I once entertained wishful ideas of changing the world, because I could see things no one else could."

I had a feeling I knew what she meant. Being someone from the outside world, a former reader of the novel, had made me special. Aria was the female lead, and Edville was the male lead. Vante and Ethen were the other potential male leads. The fact that I knew these things had given me an unreasonable amount of confidence at one point.

"But as I grew older, I realized that being different wasn't always a good thing. There were even some embarrassing incidents I'm too ashamed to talk about."

I no longer thought that way, though. During the moderate amount of time I'd been in this world, I'd realized something. Nothing was set in stone, and nothing could be taken for granted.

"I know that," I said, hanging my head. Madam Lebonae was talking about her past, but it felt like she was going over my own, and I felt embarrassed about it.

"My life wasn't a particularly amazing one worthy of admiration. But after the young man from the House of Luce told me about you, there was something I wanted to tell you." She put down the teacup she had been sipping from. "Nothing is certain in this world. There are no absolutes, no rights or wrongs. I don't know everything you've been through, my lady, but..."

I waited for her to go on.

"The life you are living now is the answer. You don't need to be afraid just because the world doesn't seem to function the way you want it to."

The words were replete with meaning. I had no idea how much she knew about me or what it was that made me look different from the other people in this world. But her words seemed to suggest that she knew far more than I'd thought.

As she said, nothing had happened the way it should have after I'd entered this world. In fact, my expectations had confused me and caused me to be lost in self-reproach. I'd only just realized that I didn't need to think this way, but getting to this point hadn't been easy. Up until a few days ago, I'd been struggling with this very topic. Thinking of Aria's face, I nodded slowly.

"Haha! At least there is hope for you, as there might be a solution." She got up and walked over to me. She stood in front of me and stared at my face. "Let's see now."

"W-what are you doing?"

Madam Lebonae reached for my face. I backed away slightly, but resistance was futile.

"As I suspected," she said, nodding and moving away.

I blinked at her, wondering what was going on. "What is this about? How am I supposed to know what you mean? You can't just run your hands over my face like that—"

"There's only one way to destroy the soul fragment remaining in your mouth," she said.

I was about to act irritated, but I fell silent, looking at her intently. *This is the very reason I came here today in the first place. To hear about this.* If I could get the answer I wanted, I would let her fumble over my face all day.

"What is it? Tell me already."

What should I do first once my tongue returns to normal? No, don't get ahead of yourself. I can do anything I want once it's fixed. I should make a list of everything I'd do.

There were so many people to see and so many things to do that my head felt like it would burst. Willing myself to calm down, I waited for her to speak.

Slowly, she said, "I don't know if you've heard of this story before..."

I gulped, staring at her lips.

"You know the old story of how a prince kissed a princess to break her curse?"

I nodded without thinking. *Is there a fairy tale about a sleeping princess in this world, too?*

"That's how it works."

I blinked, staring at her blankly when she ended her words so quickly.

"What do you mean?"

"Just like it sounds. Only the kiss of a prince can break a princess' curse," she said, tapping at her lips. "The soul fragment resides in your lips, so a kiss is the only option."

Finally understanding her, I shot to my feet. *Is she suggesting that I should kiss someone?*

"You're joking, right?"

"Why would I lie about something like this?"

If this was true, then there was no way to get rid of my condition. I felt awkward just being around Ethen. *How am I supposed to kiss him?*

"It doesn't have to be someone specific, right? Could a random stranger work... and it doesn't necessarily have to be on the lips, does it? Right? Am I right?" I rambled, my pacing quickening with my rising panic.

A kiss? That felt like an impossibility.

"It must be a kiss on the lips," she said, adding fuel to the fire. "And it's only meaningful if it's someone who loves your soul. If a random stranger could do it, what would be the point?"

What would be the point in having someone who loved me do it, then?

I wanted to deny reality. "You're lying, aren't you?"

"I can be mischievous, but I don't lie, my lady."

"This is a sick joke, right?" I said desperately, but she shook her head firmly.

"There could be other ways, perhaps. But this is the only one I know."

At her final words, I gritted my teeth, resisting the impulse to sink to the floor.

CHAPTER
ONE HUNDRED AND THIRTY-FOUR

"My lady, you're back."

I walked right past Lilian as she greeted me after I got out of my carriage. I wasn't in a mood to hold a conversation with anyone.

"Just like it sounds. Only the kiss of a prince can break a princess' curse."

"The soul fragment resides in your lips, so a kiss is the only option."

I'd finally found out how to be freed of my accursed tongue, but to think the method would be something so absurd! Perhaps it would have been better not to have found out at all.

A kiss? I never considered such a method! I touched my lips as I sat at my desk, staring blankly. It wasn't clear if I should be hopeful about this situation or the opposite.

I sighed. Less than two weeks—really, closer to a week—remained until the month I'd mentioned to Ethen would be up. He was a gentleman, and if I said nothing to him at that time, he would quietly walk away. That meant that unless I did something, Ethen and I would be broken up forever.

Not that there was much of a relationship at all to speak of... I stared at the desk with its mess of opened and unopened envelopes.

"An opportunity, huh..." I muttered under my breath.

Perhaps it was the last one I would ever have. It would be foolish of me not to grab it. But I'd been avoiding him thus far, so I wasn't feeling too enthusiastic about having to go and kiss him now. I believed it would be better to tell him how I felt, of course, than do nothing, but this method was completely unexpected. It was hard to come to a decision.

The only thing I could do right now was read the few remaining letters from Ethen.

What decision should I make to prevent both Ethen and me feeling any more miserable?

I sighed again and opened another envelope. I'd started reading in the hope it would help me organize my thoughts, but the guilt weighing me down only grew. When I was done reading them, all I could do was shut my eyes with a heavy heart.

"Mary, is something bothering you?"

Time flew by while I remained locked in my dilemma. Before I knew it, there was exactly one week remaining until the deadline.

"No."

"What do you mean, no? You have dark circles under your eyes."

I pushed at the spots below my eyes involuntarily. I did seem to remember noticing dark circles in the mirror.

"Are you sure nothing is wrong?"

"Don't worry about it. It's nothing," I said a bit hysterically, and Aria stiffened. I finally looked her in the face and hurriedly said, "There's really nothing wrong. That's all."

Though I waved my hands at her in denial, Aria already seemed to suspect I was lying. She also seemed to be hurt by the biting way I'd spoken to her.

"All right."

Instead of asking me what was wrong again, Aria clammed up. Even more disconcerted than she was by her reaction, I blinked and studied her expression.

"What?" I said cautiously. "It really is nothing."

Seeing that I wasn't apologizing or telling her the truth, Aria bit her lip for a moment and forced a smile. "Never mind. You don't have to tell me if you don't want to. Sorry if you thought I was prying." Despite her smile, she looked hurt.

"I guess we're not close enough for me to be asking such questions," seemed to be what she was thinking, and it made me uncomfortable. I couldn't bring myself to tell her, but I couldn't comfort her with affectionate words either. I wanted to tell her that I didn't think that way, that there was only so much I could say right now with my mind in such a muddle, and to apologize.

But the words that came out of my mouth were completely different. "Whatever. Don't ask if you know you are."

Don't ask if you know you are? It was a very cold thing to say. Aria looked even more hurt than before and hung her head.

I knew that continuing the conversation would not do us any good, so I quickly changed the subject. "B-but more importantly, aren't you going to rehearsals today?"

"Oh, we're rehearsing in teams today. Mine is rehearsing in the evening."

"You're getting along with the troupe members?"

"Yes. Many of them are very nice, and I've been having fun learning," she said with an effort to smile.

"And Baron Robert hasn't been tough on you?"

"He is tough... but he's like that on everyone."

That's hardly surprising, given the way he acts.

I nodded, and Aria added, "He seems to draw a clear line between work and personal life. He does get angry, but at times he gives us warm advice and even rebuked a member who tried to pick a fight with me—"

"Pick a fight with you?" I asked, not missing this slip of the tongue. *So, someone tried to bully you?* "What happened?"

"It was nothing. Nothing serious. It ended well," she said, waving her hands about as she realized her mistake.

"Tell me what it was. I'll be the judge of whether it was serious." I couldn't trust her when she said things were all right. *What if she's repressing her feelings, and things get out of hand later?*

I'd asked her firmly, but the response I got wasn't what I expected.

"No."

I couldn't believe my ears. *No? Not "it's nothing" or "it's fine," but "no?"*

"What did you say?" I asked, thinking I'd heard her wrong.

"You said you were fine, too, Mary..." she said, staring at the ground. It seemed childish, but she seemed justified in saying so. "It really is nothing. It's all been taken care of."

I was astounded at the way she distanced herself from me in exactly the same way that I had from her. I blinked, unable to say a word.

"I'm really all right."

I wondered if she had felt the same way I felt now. I bit my lip, repressing my bitter feelings.

Ethen's letters, and the hurt look on Aria's face.

As if my thoughts hadn't been convoluted enough, they grew more complicated because of those two things. I needed to do something. The current situation wasn't perfect, but at this rate, things would become irreparable.

I wished I could just march into the duke's mansion and kiss Ethen, but I lacked the courage. If I met Ethen right now, I wasn't sure what I'd even say to him. *How could I start by kissing him?*

Frustrated, I let out a sigh. *It would be nice if I could speak to someone about my concerns, at the very least.*

"Oh." A face flitted into my head.

Madam Lebonae. I can't tell her every detail either, but maybe I could share with her more than I could with anyone else.

With that thought, I got up to get ready to leave.

"My lady, are you going somewhere?"

"The same place as last time."

Annie tilted her head. "You mean the place you went with Mr. Hans?"

"Yes. It won't take long. I'll be back before Aria comes home, so don't worry."

She nodded. "Would you like me to prepare a dress?"

"Yes. Please make sure it's not a fancy one."

"Yes, my lady!" Annie said, nodding with a determined look on her face. She brought back a dress I could wear, and I was able to leave the mansion not long after the idea had entered my head.

"My lady, why are you going to the Lebonae Bakery again?" asked the horseman, who'd been called out on short notice.

"Is it any of your business?"

He lowered his head in embarrassment. "No, it's not, but that old woman is a strange person. I'm worried about you, that's all, my lady," he said hesitantly.

I guess normal people would think her strange.

"Whatever the case, she's an odd one..."

Even I was mystified by her, and I knew about her special ability. No doubt she seemed extremely unusual to those who didn't.

"Well, it's still none of your business. Get moving."

But I was just as strange as Madam Lebonae was. Strange people could understand each other, and I needed someone who could appreciate my plight right now.

"Yes, all right, my lady."

She wouldn't be able to understand me perfectly, but at least she could provide some small consolation. I stared out the window of the carriage as I thought.

The carriage arrived in front of Lebonae Bakery. It bothered me that I hadn't given her any warning, but I hoped it would be all right. After taking a deep breath, I got out of the carriage and opened the door to the bakery.

"Welcome. Oh my!" said the granddaughter, bowing to me. "What are you doing here, my lady? My grandmother isn't in right now."

"She's not?"

Not good. I frowned at this unexpected situation. "Where is she? Is she coming back today?"

"She went out for a short walk, so she probably won't be long. But she has another guest waiting," she said with a troubled look.

"Another guest?"

"Yes. You probably know him, my lady. He..."

I heard a door open behind me as she spoke.

"Lady Mary?"

"Oh my. She's back."

I turned around at the familiar voice.

"I didn't expect you to come back. Do you have something more to tell me about?" Madam Lebonae said with a chuckle, but my eyes were on the man behind her.

"Lord Vante?" *What is he doing here?* I glared at him in suspicion.

CHAPTER ONE HUNDRED AND THIRTY-FIVE

I didn't think we'd see each other here again," Vante said with a shrug.

"What are you doing here?" I asked.

"That's precisely what I'd like to ask you, Lady Mary," he said, tipping his head to the side. "Isn't that right, madam?"

"I keep telling him he doesn't need to come, but he won't listen." Madam Lebonae gave Vante an annoyed look while he smiled. Her eyes were glaring, but it was obvious that she was being playful. "He comes by now and then and helps me pass the time."

I looked at him in surprise. He was the heir to his house. I was pretty sure he couldn't have that much free time on his hands.

"Conversations get interesting when you have something in common," he said, and this allowed me to guess why he bothered to visit this out-of-the-way bakery to speak to her. Just like the reason I'd come here; he'd also felt a sense of kinship with her as someone who could see things others could not.

"It's more remarkable that you're here, Lady Mary. Where is Lady Aria? You always bring her along, don't you?"

"That's none of your business," I replied sharply, glaring at him. The mention of Aria's name put me on edge.

"But tell me, what brought you here again?" The old woman stepped into her shop. I'd come to speak to her, but I had a feeling I wouldn't be able to do so freely with Vante around.

"When are you leaving, Lord Vante?" I asked, not hiding the fact that I wanted him to leave.

Vante laughed. "Would you prefer I left right away?"

"That wouldn't be so bad," I said with a frown.

He repressed a laugh. "That just makes me want to stay more."

"You and your personality..." Madam Lebonae said, glowering playfully at him.

I looked at Vante, who smiled at me mischievously, and noticed that there was something different about him, even though he still seemed as superficial as before.

Madam Lebonae walked past him. "Do you have something to ask me?" she asked me.

"No, I just wanted to talk," I replied.

"About what?" Vante butted in.

"None of your concern," I said immediately, and he grinned.

"Who knows? Maybe I can tell you something that you'll find helpful."

I was about to brush him off and repeat my request that he leave when I started thinking. I'd come to Madam Lebonae wanting to be understood. *But isn't Vante also in a position to empathize? Maybe he could tell me something that would help.*

I nodded. "Then stay if you want," I said gruffly, and Vante smiled in satisfaction.

"Yvette, go get some tea for our guests." The old woman, who had been watching me and Vante, gestured to her granddaughter.

"Yes, Grandmother."

Moments later, an odd group was seated at the table for tea.

"Do you have something on your mind?" Madam Lebonae asked.

"Who wouldn't, after what you told me? Of course I do," I grumbled.

She looked puzzled. "It's a fine method, don't you think?"

"What makes you say that?" *How is kissing the person I've been avoiding for the longest time a good method?*

Seeing the confused look on my face, Vante asked, "What is this about?"

"Well..."

I wondered if it would be all right to tell Vante about this, but it was Madam Lebonae who responded to his question.

"I told her how to break the soul fragment that resides in her lips. But it seems the method is too hard for her to go with," she said with a shrug.

"What kind of method is it?"

"Oh, that," Madam Lebonae said without hesitation. "It's one proven by tradition. It was a prince's kiss that awakened the sleeping princess, was it not?"

"Ah..." He nodded. "What seems to be the problem, then?" he said, giving me a puzzled look.

"What?"

"The feelings are there, are they not?"

I blushed at his unexpected comment. "What are you saying?"

"Lord Ethen likes you, Lady Mary. It can't be that difficult."

It seemed like I'd been the only one who didn't know about Ethen's feelings. *How is it that everywhere I go, people seem to know?*

"How do you know that?"

"How could I not?" he said, tilting his head. "He seemed ready to bore a hole in my head with his eyes whenever I spoke to you. Given Lord Ethen's reputation for being calm, don't you think I'd think it strange?"

Did he act that way? I stared down to hide my blush and tried to remember.

I'd always been flustered when Ethen and Vante were around, so I couldn't remember all that well. It was true, though, that Ethen had helped me get rid of Vante. My assumption had been that he was only being polite as my fiancé, but perhaps that wasn't how it had seemed to others.

"And from the look of things, Lady Mary, you seem to like him, too," he said, looking at my red face.

Yes, I admit it. I like Ethen. But just because I like him doesn't mean I can go up to him and kiss him out of the blue!

"It's not a matter of how we feel. I can't try such a thing if I can't even convey my feelings properly," I said.

Vante mulled over this complicated response. "I suppose you're right. You're no ordinary person..."

This was true, but neither was Vante.

"My mistake."

"I have a question," I said to him. I was curious about something.

"What is it?"

"Doesn't it seem strange, this conversation? It's not something that's easy to believe."

Vante was suspiciously calm. *Even if he does have a special ability, how can he accept so easily that I am not the original Mary Bell and that my tongue is somehow out of my control?* It would have been normal for him to be suspicious, at the very least. But he seemed to take everything in his stride.

"You don't have to worry," he said with a quiet laugh. "Shall I tell you about what I can do? I told you last time that I have a unique ability."

I nodded. He said he could see people's colors. This hadn't been mentioned in the novel at all, which made it rather hard to believe. But then again, nothing seemed preposterous compared to my current situation.

What was more, if Vante had such an ability, it explained all the strange behavior he had exhibited so far. That made things easier to believe.

"I've never doubted my eyes, not for a moment. Having them was like having the answers to every question on a test," he said.

I nodded. I wondered if this was similar to how I'd considered my knowledge of the novel.

"That's why it was so puzzling to see you. It made no sense that a person's color could change or that someone could act contrary to that color."

I guess I would have thought the same thing in his shoes.

"That was the first time I doubted my eyes. I traveled about to test if there was a problem with my eyes or if there was something that not even my eyes could detect." He pointed to his eyes. "In hindsight, maybe it wasn't really that important. But I felt frustrated to be doubting my ability all of a sudden."

"Then he met me," Madam Lebonae cut in.

I remembered him saying that as he wandered about, testing his eyes, he'd seen Madam Lebonae—a person without color.

"After she told me that you probably weren't an ordinary person, I grew more relieved than anything else."

"Relieved?" *Why would he feel relieved about such a thing?* My head tipped in confusion.

"It seemed more plausible to me that you were someone special than that my eyes were malfunctioning. That's why I was able to believe Madam Lebonae without much difficulty."

I could understand how he'd felt. After learning about his special talent, I hadn't wondered about its veracity but rather why I hadn't read about it in the novel. Seen from this point of view, it seemed we had more in common than I'd thought. I stared at Vante, amazed at this realization. To me, he'd always been someone to avoid.

"That was why I was able to believe your story. I have no ulterior motives, so you needn't worry."

I flinched at having been read. Slowly, I said, "I didn't think that." *I did, though.* I turned my head away casually. "It must be convenient to have an ability like that."

"That's what I thought in the past," he said after taking a sip of his tea. "But I don't think that way anymore. I've learned things after getting to know Madam Lebonae."

"Haha. I didn't really teach you anything," she answered, as if his praise made her shy. "I simply told him something about life. What he took away from that is entirely his own." She smiled.

"I realized that having a unique ability is not always a good thing," Vante said after smiling back at her.

ONE HUNDRED AND THIRTY-SIX

I looked at Vante in surprise. Unlike my useless condition, seeing people's colors seemed to be a very useful ability. *What could be bad about it?*

"I don't see why that could be a bad thing. It sounds useful."

"It is," Vante agreed. "But I've learned that trusting anything too much is not a good idea."

This wasn't fortune-telling or a myth. *Why would trusting what he can see be considered bad?* I looked at him in puzzlement, his words making less and less sense as time went by.

"What we can see isn't all there is to the world. People like you must be rare, of course, but..."

He glanced at Madam Lebonae, who then continued.

"I can read people as well, but that doesn't mean I can figure them out completely."

"What, then?" I asked.

"People don't always live according to the way they were born. When I was younger, I believed that our futures were set in stone and considered myself to be a very wise person," she said, deep in thought.

"It's an amazing ability, isn't it? I thought the same thing. Because I could detect people's energy, I believed I could figure out a person in mere seconds."

There was a complicated mix of emotions on her face. "It was a naive way of thinking, of course. The way a person has lived their life matters just as much as inborn traits."

I was reminded of a few things when I heard her words—things that had happened with Aria, Ethen, Edville, and Iris. They couldn't fundamentally be different people from the people they had been in the novel, but their lives were completely different now.

"I considered my ability perfect, but then I made a huge mistake. I decided then that I would tell nobody about what I could see." She dropped her gaze. "But I couldn't stand back and do nothing when I saw you young people who seemed so similar to the way I'd been in my youth. Hence my meddling."

"But I don't have the ability to see things like you can." What I had couldn't even be called an ability—more like a curse.

"Even if you can't see anything, thinking you know everything is a dangerous thing," she said, her words full of meaning. "I don't know what scares you so much, but there must be a reason you came back." She took my hand and stared into my eyes. "This is the world you must live in. There is nothing to be afraid of or taken for granted. That's why you don't need to fear approaching this person."

Is this really true? Can I really think that way? I looked at Madam Lebonae with uncertainty.

She nodded. "You can come to me at any time if you need someone to talk to. I have more time than I know what to do with. There might be unwelcome guests on some days, of course, like today..."

"Unwelcome? That's not fair," Vante grumbled, then he turned to look at me. "If you're fine with me, I can also lend an ear. But if you want, I'll leave."

"Come now. You should have said that much earlier if you meant it," Madam Lebonae teased.

They couldn't have known each other for that long, but there seemed to be a strong bond between them. A laugh escaped my lips as I looked at them.

"Haha. All right, then." The impudent laughter I was so used to now rang out in the bakery, and they gently smiled back.

"I hope you can achieve what you wish for. That way, Lord Ethen will stop glaring at me whenever I see him," Vante said playfully.

I burst out laughing again.

Yes. There's no need to be afraid. Nothing is set in stone, nothing is predestined. Maybe there is something I can say with these lips. So don't be so anxious.

I decided not to be so afraid. I hadn't had such a positive thought in days.

"Is that true?"

Ever since Mary had been to the Lebonae Bakery, strange rumors had begun to spread among the servants of the marquess' mansion.

"Of course. Mr. Hans saw her."

"But how?"

"He's basically her personal horseman these days. Didn't you see him drive her out yesterday?"

The maids at the mansion were chatting among themselves while hanging out the laundry. This in itself was not a rare occurrence, but their topic of conversion was.

"To think she's got something going on with Lord Vante! That can't be right."

"I know, right? After Lord Ethen was so good to her, too…"

"But that doesn't guarantee affection, does it? And she's so fickle, too. It's surprising that she liked him for so long, ever since she was a child."

The source of the rumor was none other than Hans, the horseman. He hadn't gone around saying that Mary and Vante were having an affair, though.

"Where have you been?"

"A bakery in an alleyway. I drove Lady Mary there."

"A bakery in an alleyway? But she already has a favorite bakery, doesn't she? Why go to one in a secluded alleyway, even if she wanted to try out another one?"

It had started when he'd had a conversation with the other attendants. People had been pitying him lately because of the recent accident. He'd wanted to tell people that Lady Mary had forgiven him, and by saying some unnecessary things, he'd inadvertently started some rumors.

"I don't know for sure, but she was meeting someone there."

"A friend?"

"No. It was a man."

Hans hadn't stopped to consider the waves his words might make.

"What did he look like?"

"A handsome lord with silver hair and purple eyes."

Hans had no idea that Mary had met Lord Vante. He'd guessed that the man was a noble from the way he acted and from his clothes, but he hadn't given much thought to the matter beyond that.

A handsome lord with silver hair and purple eyes...

But one of the servants who'd heard him was different. He was in charge of guiding guests to the parties that Lady Mary held so often. Silver hair and purple eyes were not at all common, so it wasn't hard for him to guess who Mary had met.

"They seemed to enjoy each other's company. Lady Mary laughed as she spoke," Hans had said chattily, having completely forgotten that an old woman had been with them. He'd only intended to show off the fact that the lady trusted him enough to let him know about her personal dealings, but the story grew in scope as it was passed around.

"Lady Mary met Lord Vante yesterday, I hear."

"They'd already been writing each other, from what I heard."

"My goodness, is there something going on between them?"

The rumors were getting out of hand.

"Lady Mary has been meeting Lord Vante in secret."

"I heard that she ran out of the mansion the moment she got his letter."

"They were supposedly looking at each other so lovingly. Lady Mary never had such a look on her face before!"

Before long, the servants of the mansion believed that they were lovers. Some of them went to Lilian, Anna, and Annie, Mary's personal maids, to confirm this.

"What?"

"It's nothing."

The maids, unable to bring themselves to ask Lilian, shifted their target.

"Anna, have you heard anything?"

"I've been too preoccupied with helping Lady Aria recently..."

Anna had nothing to tell the others because she knew nothing. Annie was the problem.

"Annie, haven't you been waiting on her these days?"

Annie clammed up, remembering that Mary had told her not to speak of her visits to anyone.

"You really don't know where Lady Mary is?"

"I can't say anything." She'd meant to say she couldn't say anything because she'd promised Lady Mary, but silence could be interpreted in a lot of ways.

The maids, convinced they were right, looked at each other and nodded.

"Why are you asking things like this? You never ask such questions," Annie said to them, confused by the barrage of questions. Nobody in the mansion wanted to be Mary's personal maid, and the other maids tended to avoid asking about her to avoid any chance of association. "You aren't even interested in Lady Mary."

"Don't say that. That's not fair. You can't tell us anything, right?" said a maid, having completed a fictional account in her head.

"No. But why—"

"No, forget it. We won't say you told us anything, so don't worry. See you."

The maids believed Annie would get into trouble if Mary heard she had talked about her, and they were being nice in their own way.

Annie had basically given the rumor wings, but for some time after, she didn't realize what she'd done. The rumor spread to every servant in the mansion but Mary's personal maids, and in less than a day, it had spread beyond its walls.

Such rumors always reached the people involved the slowest—but someone else heard about it first.

"Ah, is that so?"

Ethen lowered his pen, a wry look on his face.

CHAPTER
ONE HUNDRED AND THIRTY-SEVEN

The rumor that had begun in the marquess' mansion had reached Ethen the morning after Mary had met Vante. A maid who'd been going about town on her day off had talked to her younger sister, igniting the spread of the rumor.

"That's right. The horseman said he saw it himself. And her personal maid refuses to say anything. What do you think that means? There's definitely something going on."

"My goodness, I've heard some nobles lead very promiscuous lives, but this..."

As it happened, Heint was also in town and overheard someone else talking about this. It was when he was waiting for his carriage after running some errand that he heard the ringing tones of a maid's voice.

"My goodness, I thought she was engaged to Lord Ethen?"

Heint had not thought much of this at first, but the name of his liege stopped him in his tracks. There was something very suspicious about the conversation, and he couldn't ignore it after hearing his master's name.

He immediately charged at the maid and grabbed her arm. "What are you talking about?"

"What?" said the woman, shocked to have a stranger grab her on the arm. "W-who are you?"

"Ah." Heint came to his senses and let go of her. "My apologies. I'm a steward who works at the House of Frangert."

"Oh…" The woman turned pale. Why had a steward of the House of Frangert, of all people, overheard the conversation? She looked panicked, then tried to run. "I-I'm sorry. I have something urgent to attend to—"

"No. I don't want your apology. I'd like to know more about what you were just saying," Heint said resolutely.

He didn't seem like he would let her go until she told him. Cursing her luck, she said, "It's nothing. Just a rumor going around among the servants."

"I would still like to hear it for myself," he said, blocking her way. If this had to do with Lady Mary's personal life, he had to hear it.

"Is that letter for Lady Mary again?"

"Yes."

Heint sent letters to the marquess' mansion every single day, but he knew that his liege had never gotten a single reply.

"I don't need a reply. I'm just expressing my feelings. And it would be terrible if I happened to miss a day and she intended to reply on that day, wouldn't it?"

But the woman that his liege loved so much was actually seeing someone else? Even if it was an unfounded rumor, Heint couldn't pass it up.

"I-it's a baseless rumor. I don't believe it to be true either," the maid said, looking very much afraid.

Heint could tell what she feared. "I won't tell anyone who I heard it from," he said, nodding. "I don't know your name or your station."

Only then did the woman speak. "Well... Lady Mary met Lord Vante yesterday, you see."

Lord Vante? Heint knew of him. Ethen was openly hostile toward the man. And what was more, there had once been rumors that he was interested in Lady Mary. Trying to ignore the anxiety that washed over him, he waited for the maid to continue.

"I don't know why they met or what their relationship is, but some say that they looked quite close."

Heint shut his eyes. This was not a good sign. She was openly avoiding her fiancé, Ethen, but met with a man who had shown such open interest in her as to be rude. Anyone who thought nothing of this would be a fool.

"B-but I'm sure this doesn't mean anything." She was trying to keep the conversation from getting too serious, but neither she nor Heint seemed to really believe this. If people had been speaking of this out in the open, they had to believe it to be a fact. He opened his eyes.

"We've been telling each other it can't be true. She has Lord Ethen, so how—"

"Thank you for telling me," Heint said, bowing with a sad look on his face.

He'd been somewhat upset that Mary wasn't responding to his master's letters, but he hadn't guessed something of this sort could have happened. He wondered if he should tell Ethen about it or not. He would be shocked—but hiding it didn't seem to be an option.

"May I leave now?" said the maid, growing more and more nervous as Heint stood there thinking. She'd told him because he'd looked ready to go to the marquess' mansion to ask if she didn't, but he seemed to be taking this far more seriously than she'd expected. *What if he decides to go to the marquess' mansion and find out if it is true?*

Heint figured there was no point in making the maid stay any longer when she knew nothing more. He did his best to smile. "Thank you for telling me. I can't keep you here forever."

"Please don't tell Lord Ethen about me—"

"I won't. Please don't worry."

The woman nodded anxiously. "If you'll excuse me." She looked around as if someone was coming after her and walked away.

Heint sighed deeply. He had been on an errand for the head steward but had heard something far too shocking.

"Lord Vante of all people..."

What would Lord Ethen say if he heard of this? But Heint couldn't keep silent after what he'd heard, either. The problem would grow even worse if Ethen heard about the rumor later, after it had spread further.

"How am I supposed to tell him?"

He trod toward the duke's mansion with heavy footsteps. When he arrived at the mansion, he told Ethen about what he'd heard.

Ethen's first reaction was to give a hollow laugh. He seemed to have been expecting this, and Heint flinched.

"Ah, is that so?" Ethen put down his pen with a complicated look on his face. He bit his lip gently and lapsed into thought.

There was only a week left before the deadline. So far, Ethen had tried everything he could. He'd sent letters every day and striven to make a good impression at the party his mother had hosted. Mary had never reciprocated, but he had been thankful that there was something he could try, at the very least.

But perhaps it was never meant to work out. It felt extremely disconcerting that Mary had gone to see another man.

"Should I look into this further?" Heint said cautiously. His liege hadn't looked particularly happy over the past month, but this look of despair was something new.

"No... that's all right."

Would it be a good thing to learn more? Would it hurt even more? Ethen hung his head. *Why is it Lord Vante, of all people?* He'd had a bad feeling about the man from the beginning.

Ethen picked up his pen again and started scribbling circles on the paper. He hadn't liked the man from the first time he'd met him. He'd approached Mary rudely and spoken to her brazenly, even though her fiancé was right next to her.

Was he interested in Mary all along? That in itself was offensive, but there was something else that made him even more uncomfortable.

"Does she prefer that kind of man...?"

Vante was Ethen's polar opposite. Ethen was a man of few words, and he was prudent. He was cautious to the point of being frustrating and was always polite toward Mary.

Vante, on the other hand, was a very forward man. There was a hidden reason behind his attitude, of course, but Ethen had no way of knowing that.

Ethen wondered if he should have acted the same way. Should he have been bolder even if it would have embarrassed him? He laughed in self-mockery. Perhaps none of this had any meaning now.

"You're still engaged. We can't have such rumors going around. Should I do something about it?" Heint asked carefully.

Ethen considered, then said, "Go and find out."

The pen broke under his fingers. It was difficult to tell if he was angry or simply anxious as he put down the broken pen. Though he'd thought moments ago that ignorance might hurt less, he felt that knowing the truth would be better than staying in the dark. Maybe the truth would help him see reason.

"I'm sorry?"

"Find out how the rumor spread and what their relationship really is," Ethen said in a low voice. There was less than a week remaining for him. There was a chance that he might have to face an unpleasant truth even before that time was up. "Get all the details and report back to me."

Maybe it would be best if he could give up on her after learning the truth. That's what was on his mind as he ordered

Heint. He had slept fitfully over the past month or so, and it seemed tonight would be no different.

It took less than a day for Ethen, sitting at his desk and unable to focus on his documents, to hear something more about the rumor.

At about the same time, the person directly involved learned of the rumor as well.

CHAPTER
ONE HUNDRED AND THIRTY-EIGHT

"My lady, I realize this may seem rude, but allow me to ask you a question." Lilian came to me at lunchtime that day with a grave look on her face. I'd finished a slightly early lunch and had been thinking about how to respond to Ethen's letters when she suddenly came into my room.

"What is it?"

She was never the expressive type, but there was something resolutely determined about her today, and I realized something had to be wrong.

What exactly put such a look on Lilian's face? I hardly do anything these days, so I couldn't have made trouble. I nodded as I searched my memory.

Lilian slowly said, "Are you seeing someone else besides Lord Ethen?"

I coughed violently, choking from the shock. As I struggled to catch my breath, I tried to process what I'd just heard.

"What do you mean?"

"Please be honest, my lady."

What is this about? Confused, I said, "What are you even talking about?"

Seeing someone else besides Ethen? That's pure insanity. I couldn't begin to guess where such a baseless rumor had started.

"Please give me a clear answer to this first. Is it really not true?"

"Why would I do such a thing?" I asked indignantly. *Do I seem the sort to be unfaithful?*

Lilian looked relieved. "So... it's not true, then."

"Of course it isn't. Who suggested such a thing?" I asked, putting down my pen.

Lilian, back to her usual calm self, said, "Let me ask you a few more things before I tell you. Where did you go yesterday?"

I'd been to the Lebonae Bakery yesterday. It wasn't something I was looking to hide, but I frowned, knowing that she'd ask me why I'd gone to such a random place.

"Must I tell you that?"

"Yes, you must." Lilian nodded firmly, her expression serious.

Did something really happen? "I went to a bakery in an alleyway for personal reasons," I said, looking displeased.

"It wasn't for a tryst?"

A tryst?! I gave her another flabbergasted look. "Who's been telling you these stupid things? The horseman could tell you that I met a white-haired old woman."

"An old woman?"

"Yes. Are you suggesting she is my lover?"

Noting my aggressive tone, Lilian appeared relieved. "There seems to be some sort of misunderstanding."

"What misunderstanding?"

"People in the mansion have been saying you've been seeing a lover in secret."

What? But why? I thought about what I'd done yesterday. I'd taken the horseman Hans and gone to the Lebonae Bakery. Hans must have seen me speaking with Madam Lebonae.

One wall of the bakery is made of glass, which means he must have seen... Huh? Don't tell me...

I looked up. An ominous feeling came over me. "Are you talking about Lord Vante?"

"Yes..."

I was starting to see what had happened. No doubt Hans had remembered seeing Vante far better than Madam Lebonae. He must have talked about it, and that must have started the rumors.

"How absurd. I went to the bakery for a different reason. It was a coincidence that I met Lord Vante there."

"Are you sure?"

"Yes. Why would I lie to you?"

Lilian explained the rumor to me. "I overheard some maids talking among themselves, and when I asked them what it was about, they said they'd heard from the horseman."

It was as I'd suspected. Hans had started it.

"It's true that I saw him, but why would I have gone there just to meet him? I don't even know him that well," I said, nonplussed. It was incredible that such a rumor had gone around after only a short conversation with him. I couldn't understand it.

"Most of the servants are aware that Lord Ethen sends letters every single day. A few know that you haven't responded to a single one," Lilian said evenly. "And when it became known that Annie refused to answer when the maids asked her a question, the rumors seemed to have gained credibility."

"Annie?"

What question did she avoid? I tilted my head in confusion.

"They asked her if she knew where you'd been, and Annie simply refused to respond instead of denying it."

Oh, she'd been unnecessarily loyal. I remembered how Annie had nodded at me, saying that I didn't have to worry about a thing. I'd only asked her to keep it a secret because I couldn't be bothered to answer questions.

Who knew this would happen? Making a face, I rested my palm against my forehead.

"Annie seems to have reacted that way because she was unaware of the rumors... but as a result, everyone seems to believe you were there to see Lord Vante."

"That's nonsense. Go tell everyone that I wasn't looking to meet him and that I'm not interested in him at all," I said, shaking my head. Things would get troublesome if other people started hearing about this.

"I'll do that. But I think you'll have to come out here right away."

"Why should I?"

I don't have to tell the servants myself, do I? Even if I did, there would still be people who refused to believe. *Why is she telling me to do this?*

I looked at her in confusion, and she responded quietly, "The master has heard about the rumor."

I froze, my mouth wide open.

"Mary, I respect your decision, whatever it may be... But there's a correct order to everything, isn't there?" my father said in a gentle voice.

I sat in front of him, looking guilty, but then my indignation took over. "No."

"Huh?" He seemed to believe that I'd already moved on to a new relationship with Vante.

I corrected him. "I only met Lord Vante by accident. There's nothing going on between us."

"Really?" He brightened. Though he said he'd respect my decision, it seemed he had still been worried.

"I know about the stupid rumor you've heard, but it isn't true. I have no idea why people have been talking like that," I said with a shudder.

I could see my father's face relaxing little by little. But he looked doubtful again and asked cautiously, "Then how did you end up meeting him?"

"I went to meet someone else, a white-haired old woman. If you go and ask Hans right now, that's what he'll tell you." I shrugged. "He probably only remembered Lord Vante and mentioned him."

"Then... may I ask why you went to see that old woman?" my father asked carefully.

I gave him the answer I'd been thinking about the entire time I walked to his office. "She helped Aria once, so I went to thank her." I felt guilty about using Aria as my excuse, but it couldn't be helped. I gulped. "I don't have to explain my actions to everyone, do I? That's why I told my maid not to speak of it."

"I see," my father said, visibly relieved. "I knew you wouldn't do such a thing, but rumors can be scary." He tried to comfort me, but he wasn't very convincing. "I knew something would need to be done if it turned out to be true. That's why I asked. I hope you aren't offended."

"Don't worry about that," I said, trying to comfort him back.

He glanced at me nervously. "I've heard Lord Ethen has been writing you every day."

My face hardened a little as I looked at him.

"I don't mean to pry, but... apparently you haven't been writing him back that often," he said, trying his best not to offend me. "As I've told you before, I will respect any decision you make. If you're not interested in him anymore, it's not necessary to continue the engagement. Of course, it wouldn't be proper to start a new relationship before this one is over," he added in a small voice. "If that's what this is..."

"No," I said with a heavy heart. "I was too busy to respond, that's all. You know I've had a lot to handle. And you don't have to worry about my relationship with him. I was just about to answer his letters."

My father looked surprised. "Oh. I'm sorry, I didn't mean to interrupt."

If my ever-busy father had heard about this, it was safe to assume everyone else knew.

Including Ethen.

"But Mary, as I've told you before, don't force yourself into anything you don't want. All your mother and I want is for you to be happy." He smiled at me. "Do whatever makes you happy. Right now, you make us proud with your accomplishments, but even if you accomplished nothing, we would still love you." He took my hand, apparently wanting to make up for his mistake, but I could see he meant what he said. "Just be true to yourself."

True to myself? After hearing his words of encouragement, I spoke on impulse. "I was planning to go to the duke's mansion tomorrow, actually. Then these stupid rumors will die down."

A decision I wouldn't be ashamed of. I didn't know what that would be exactly, but I could now be sure of one thing. Hiding like a coward wouldn't change anything, and there was nothing more shameful than doing nothing. It was time for me to end this frustrating situation once and for all, regardless of what I'd have to do.

CHAPTER ONE HUNDRED AND THIRTY-NINE

As soon as I returned to my room after the conversation with my father, I sat at my desk. There was only a week left until the deadline I'd mentioned—no, less than that. If I hesitated any longer, the month would be over before I could do anything.

I didn't want that to happen.

After taking a deep breath, I started writing without hesitation.

"Annie, are you there?"

"Yes, my lady." Annie entered cautiously, seemingly having heard the rumor belatedly. "My lady, I—"

"Just take this," I said, cutting her short as she tried to explain herself. I extended my hand, holding out an envelope without further explanation.

"My lady?"

"Send this to the duke's mansion. I think it'd be great if you told everyone that I just sent a reply."

My father and Lilian had learned the truth, so they would soon correct the rumor. But sometimes a single action could do more to mend the situation than a thousand explanations.

"You don't have to look so guilty. I told you to keep it a secret, and you did what I requested, didn't you? I won't tell you off for it. What do you take me for?"

"My lady..." Annie said, looking touched.

I avoided her eyes, which were glowing and making me feel uncomfortable. "And I'll be going to the duke's mansion tomorrow, so keep that in mind," I said firmly.

The letter was brief, its contents simple, so writing it took little time.

There is about a week left until the month is up, but I am writing to you now because I have something I need to tell you. It is probably best if we meet for this. May I come and see you tomorrow?

Though I was asking for permission, I knew that he wouldn't refuse. Despite being such a busy person, he'd never once refused me when I asked to meet.

"The duke's mansion?" Annie asked in surprise. Then she nodded with a determined look on her face.

I sighed quietly. Tomorrow would be the day I ended this frustrating situation. It might not end with the best-case scenario—my mouth returning to normal—but I couldn't let this drag on for much longer.

I knew that I needed to speak to him face to face.

Ethen sat at his desk with a letter to one side and Heint in front of him. But he was looking at neither.

A troubled expression crossed his face as he urged, "Tell me."

"Yes. First of all, it seems to be true that Lady Mary met with Lord Vante," Heint said, unable to look Ethen in the eye. "The horseman confirmed that they spoke and that they seemed to be enjoying the conversation."

"Just the two of them?"

Heint considered all the rumors he'd collected. "I can't be sure. But that's probably the case. The horseman would have remembered if there had been more people involved." What was more, their meeting location was odd as well. Heint added, as he thought about it, "Though I don't know for certain, I think it's likely they were alone."

A bitter smile formed on Ethen's face.

So, it is true, then?

The last time Vante and Mary had met, the two of them hadn't looked to be on great terms. *When did this relationship develop? At the hunting competition? No, that can't be the case.* Mary had despised him back then.

Did it happen after she told me of her intent to call off the engagement, then? Maybe it was sometime between that point and the hunting competition.

Made nervous by the various possibilities, he shook his head to clear his anxious thoughts.

"Shouldn't you read the letter?" Heint said cautiously. He was never a tactful person, but today he couldn't help being careful.

"All right." Ethen reached for the letter with a heavy heart. This was the first response she'd given him since the formal reply she'd sent regarding the duchess' party.

What could be in this letter? Why did it arrive right after I'd heard the rumors about Lord Vante? And why did this rumor reach me so quickly? He felt that everything seemed to suggest that the two of them weren't meant to be. He bit his lip anxiously.

But he couldn't avoid reading the letter. He took a paper knife and opened the seal.

There is about a week left until the month is up, but I am writing to you now because I have something I need to tell you.

It had taken a while for him to work up the courage to read it, but it only took him a moment to finish it. Ethen gave a quiet laugh, realizing that the length of the letter seemed to indicate just how uninterested Mary was in him.

Heint tensed upon hearing his laugh. *What made him laugh like that? It can't be good, whatever it is. Is she calling off the engagement?*

Assuming the worst, Heint poked his head out and tried to peek. He couldn't see the words very well, but it was clear the letter was very short. *Huh? Why is it so short?*

If the letter was about breaking things off, it likely wouldn't be so terse. *No, maybe it would be.* Imagining various things in his mind, Heint tried to guess what was written in the letter. He was silent for some time as he considered it, then noticed that Ethen was still quiet, staring at the letter.

"Are you feeling all right, my lord?"

"Why wouldn't I be?" Ethen said, shaking his head. He looked far from all right. Moments later, he finally put the letter down. "There isn't much in the letter."

"Is it something difficult to talk about?" Heint asked with a gulp.

Another light laugh escaped Ethen's lips. "No. She asked if she could visit tomorrow. She has something to tell me face to face."

What could it be about? Heint quivered, suddenly feeling anxious. "That's it?"

"Yes. I guess I'll find out tomorrow what this is about."

Ethen took out a piece of paper and began to write a reply. It was a short letter, so the response probably didn't need to be long. Though he usually wrote about his daily life, concerns, and various other topics, he couldn't seem to think of any ordinary subjects today.

You are always welcome to visit. Please come in the afternoon for tea. I will be waiting.

He'd been about to politely write that he was looking forward to the conversation, but he paused and thought better of it, simply writing that he'd be waiting instead. Having taken considerable time writing those three sentences, Ethen folded up the letter, put it in an envelope, and sealed it with the family seal.

It occurred to him that this might be the last letter he would be sending her. He held the letter out to Heint.

"Send it to the marquess' mansion."

He did his best to stay composed, but his shaking hand gave him away. Heint took the letter.

"It's probably nothing important. She's probably only just found the time in her busy schedule to respond. The lady she's been sponsoring has performed at Lady Priscilla's concert recently, you know," Heint said, trying to set Ethen's mind at ease. "She was probably too busy with that to respond to you so far. It was only by coincidence that I learned of the rumor. She probably doesn't know that you heard about it as well."

Heint's words were a mixture of wishful thinking and partial truth, but he couldn't stop himself. The look on Ethen's face was too dark.

"I've heard that she's also working with the imperial theater. She is surely busy."

"You think so?" Ethen said, nodding, though he didn't really agree.

"It probably has nothing to do with Lord Vante. Please don't be concerned," Heint said. He tried to comfort Ethen with hopeful words, but neither Ethen nor Heint believed them. "There's no need to worry."

But there was something Heint didn't know. Mary had already told Ethen she wanted to call off the engagement, and the reprieve he'd childishly forced from her was coming to an end.

"It's probably nothing serious, and you'll forget about it after tomorrow."

If Heint had known of this, he probably wouldn't have been as hopeful as he was now. Ethen gave a quiet laugh.

"You agree, don't you?" Heint smiled, assuming Ethen had accepted the consolation.

It would be best if one of them, at least, didn't have to worry. Ethen nodded. "Yes. I think you might be right."

"I'll send the letter and inform the head steward that Lady Mary will be visiting tomorrow." Heint looked happy, thinking he'd succeeded in setting Ethen's mind at ease.

Ethen sighed deeply once Heint had left the room. He couldn't bring himself to believe that Mary's news would be good. In the worst-case scenario, she'd tell him she'd started a new relationship with Vante. Even if that wasn't the case, he couldn't picture tomorrow's conversation ending well. How could he be optimistic when there was less than a week left, and they hadn't been able to meet very often over the course of the month?

Ethen pulled the documents he hadn't been able to focus on all day closer to him to stop himself from thinking of Mary. He wanted a distraction. This relationship would be over by tomorrow, no matter what she wanted to talk about. Maybe that was for the best. It would hurt, but at least he would no longer have to suffer from a cruel hope.

With that thought, he glued his eyes on the documents.

CHAPTER
ONE HUNDRED AND FORTY

Anxiety kept Ethen awake all through the night.

Of course, it wasn't that he didn't try. Every time he was reminded of Mary, he got up and picked up documents to try to drown out his thoughts with work. Before long, the sun had risen.

He put a hand to his forehead, dark circles under his eyes. Though he'd tried so hard to keep her out of his thoughts, he hadn't really succeeded.

Knock, knock.

"My lord, are you awake?" Heint called from outside the door. He had probably gone to Ethen's bedroom to wake him, and finding that he was gone, come over to the office right away.

"You're up early," Heint said, walking up to him. Thinking Ethen must have gotten up earlier than usual, he reached for the documents Ethen had looked over. Then he noticed Ethen's appearance and flinched.

"You got up early... right?" Heint asked, but Ethen turned away. "You stayed up all night?" It was more of a statement than a question.

Ethen didn't respond, and Heint sighed. "You've handled all these documents. Please get some rest. There are still a few hours until Lady Mary arrives," he said, looking at the clock.

Heint was right. Mary was going to arrive after lunch. Though Ethen wouldn't be able to rest fully, it was still morning, and there was time for a nap. Heint tried to take the pen out of Ethen's hand.

"That won't be necessary. I'm not even tired."

Not very convincing, considering the state of your face, Heint thought, shaking his head. But he knew that Ethen was not easily dissuaded, so he gave up on convincing him to do otherwise.

"You should eat, then, at the very least. Lady Mary will be shocked to see you like this."

This seemed to give Ethen a jolt. He rubbed his face. "All right..." Mary had liked his looks—if nothing else. "This might be the last time we meet. I can't meet her looking exhausted." He got up from his seat.

"The last time? Please don't say things like that," Heint clamored after him, but Ethen trudged out without a word.

Ethen stood in front of the mirror, turning this way and that as he checked his appearance. Just last month, he'd been excited as he prepared in front of the mirror to meet Mary. But today, he didn't feel that way at all.

Now, he felt like a lamb being led to the slaughter.

However, considering this might be the last time, he didn't want to meet Mary in an unpresentable state. Although there was quite some time left until Mary was to arrive, he stood there nervously, trying to spruce himself up.

"You look great already. I think you've been standing there long enough," Heint finally said.

Ethen was wearing his best clothes and had neatened up his appearance, but he had been standing there for over thirty minutes. Heint was frustrated by the way Ethen kept touching up his hair and changing into various clothes—all of which looked fine—and staring nervously at his reflection.

"It won't matter to her much what clothes you're wearing," Heint said, meaning that she would simply be happy to see him, but to the anxious Ethen, this sounded quite different.

I guess he's right. If her mind is made up, what does it matter how I look?

Seeing Ethen's shoulders droop noticeably, Heint stared at his liege nervously, wondering if he'd said something wrong. "I-I just meant that she'll like you no matter what you wear," he added, but the damage had already been done.

Ethen glanced at the mirror again, hating the sight of himself for some reason. Though he'd tried to hide them, the dark circles under his eyes were still there, and his lips were chapped and bleeding because he'd picked at them in his apprehension. There wasn't a single thing he liked about himself at the moment.

"How much longer now?" Ethen mumbled.

Heint realized what he was asking without much difficulty. "I think she'll be here in about thirty minutes."

That wasn't a long time. Ethen stopped checking himself in the mirror and left. "Let's go."

He walked toward the garden so that he could get ready to greet Mary. He'd hurriedly purchased and placed Mary's favorite flowers, roses, throughout the garden. It might prove to be meaningless, but he wanted Mary to remember the day fondly, even if it was the last. He'd already instructed the servants to make the preparations perfect, but he headed to the garden anyway, unable to rest easily.

He'd met Mary so many times in this garden. The meetings had been obligatory and formal at first, but past a certain point, he'd started looking forward to them and even waited desperately for them. And now he was dealing with the conflicting urges to stay and run away at the same time.

He rested his hands on the table where Mary would soon sit and settled into recollection. This was where Mary had asked to call off the engagement, and in the greatest act of bravery he'd ever performed, he'd asked her for a reprieve. Had he been certain he could make her stay; he would have given up on his pride and begged her all over again. But he wasn't certain at all.

What happened to the wreath I gave her that day? She might have thrown it away, as she hadn't looked so happy to receive it.

"I guess I'll end up just like that wreath," he said with a wry smile.

He sat there, recollecting the conversations he'd had with her at this table, for a while.

Before long, Heint appeared. He seemed to have been looking for Ethen. "My lord, Lady Mary's carriage has arrived."

Is it time already? Ethen moved his hands off the table. "Let's go, then."

The entrance where the carriage had stopped wasn't too far from the garden. He stepped out of the garden so that he could welcome her, and he saw the familiar carriage in the distance. A beautiful woman with red hair stepped out.

"Good afternoon, Lady Mary." Hiding his fear, Ethen walked up to her. He was trying to seem normal, but he wasn't sure how his voice actually sounded.

"Yes, good afternoon," Mary answered.

There was something different about her today. She'd always seemed awkward around him, but there was a resolute look on her face this time.

"I prepared a seat in the garden since you seemed to like it last time."

"Oh, that wasn't necessary," Mary said, her eyes widening.

Does she have so little to say that sitting in the garden isn't necessary?

Ethen gulped and forced himself to smile. "May I escort you?" he said, holding out his hand.

Mary stared at it for a moment, as if to decide whether she should take it. "Thank you," she said after a short moment, placing her hand on his.

Ethen grabbed it lightly and led her to the garden. It was approaching fall, but there were roses everywhere. There weren't that many, because he'd bought them in a hurry, but they showed the effort he'd put in.

"It's beautiful," Mary said quietly.

He smiled faintly, pleased that it had been worth it, at least. "I'm relieved."

They arrived at the table, and Ethen sat down after pulling out her chair for her. A maid appeared with a tray and placed some refreshments on the table.

"The chef said he would do his best to please you again with his food."

"I see. These look amazing."

Ethen was doing his best to hide his anxiety, but his lips were quivering as he smiled.

"It's starting to get cold," he said. "If I'd known, I would have arranged for tea inside. Maybe you'd like to go inside—" He covered his lips. He thought it would probably be better to pretend to be cold than to let on that he was nervous.

"It's all right. It's only fall; I can stand this kind of weather," Mary said simply.

It was difficult to tell if she'd noticed. She was right. It wasn't too cold for tea at three in the afternoon.

"Is that so? Good to hear," Ethen said, lowering his hand awkwardly.

And for some time, silence fell between them. They sipped their tea, and the cozy but cool fall breeze blowing between them felt like the calm before a storm.

"That day..." she said, breaking the silence.

Ethen's hand trembled, but he quickly smiled as if he hadn't been startled at all. "Yes."

"I felt uncomfortable about leaving so suddenly without saying a proper goodbye," she said, offering a belated apology.

"Don't mention it. My mother wasn't concerned at all. In fact—"

"She spoke to the House of Mirvaseba as well." She finished his sentence.

Ethen was surprised. He'd thought Mary hadn't read any of his letters—because she never replied. But it seemed she'd at least read them.

"Yes. I was told the countess promised to have a stern word with her daughter. So please don't worry about it."

"How could I not, when it has to do with me?" Mary took a deep breath. She seemed to have reached some kind of momentous decision.

"I'm here to speak to you about what we agreed on a month ago."

CHAPTER ONE HUNDRED AND FORTY-ONE

What we agreed on a month ago.

This had to be about calling off their engagement. *So, she is here to talk about that after all.* Ethen had been prepared for it, but hearing it made his heart sink.

He bit his lip. "Yes."

"It hasn't been a full month yet, but I think it's best I tell you in advance."

Every word felt like another stone added to the weight pulling him under. Ethen did his best to shake off his anxiety and answer her. "Understood."

He'd assumed the worst all night, while he'd been unable to sleep. He'd imagined over and over again what it would feel like and how sharp her words would be. All his ruminations paled in comparison to reality. Though she'd said nothing specific yet, his heart was already racing. If things were this bad already, perhaps he'd have a heart attack by the end of the conversation.

He waited for her to continue.

"I've been doing a lot of thinking over the past month. As you know, something unpleasant happened during that time." She seemed to be referring to the incident with Iris.

Ethen nodded. It took him a lot of effort to talk about a casual topic. "But good things happened as well. I've heard that Lady Aria sang at Lady Priscilla's performance." He knew that the topic he was dreading was unavoidable, but he wanted to delay it as much as possible.

He forced a smile. "You seemed happy when you saw Lady Priscilla's performance last time. You must be proud that Lady Aria has improved to the point of performing with her."

"It's her achievement, not mine... but I was happy, yes." Mary's lips relaxed a little. This was the most at ease she'd been since she got out of the carriage with a determined look on her face.

"It should be a good thing for the imperial theater that's opening soon," he said.

"Yes. They received the best possible advertising for free," she said with a laugh.

Seeing her smile again allowed him to lay down his fears for a moment and smile back.

"They told us that she couldn't perform on stage without having something to show for herself first, so we taught them a lesson." She sounded somewhat excited. This was the Mary that Ethen loved the most. The Mary who loved her work.

"It would have been nice if you had come along…" Mary said, forgetting herself for a moment. But she caught herself and continued, "You would have been impressed, too, if you'd seen it." She soon recovered her composure, and the comfortable air that had existed between them vanished again, as though it had never existed.

"Yes. I'm sure I would have." Ethen bowed his head, feeling the bitter aftertaste of the fleeting moment. "Please tell Lady Aria I congratulated her."

"Thank you," she said, looking mildly embarrassed. "In any case… I'd like to meet with the duchess and speak with her properly next time."

"Then I can tell my mother—"

"No. I'll contact her myself," she said firmly.

This made his heart sink again. Mary seemed to be perfectly aware of what she was here to do. Her every word carried conviction, and whatever decision she had made, he had the feeling there was no reversing it. *Is there really nothing I can do?*

"I have something else to talk to you about." She looked him in the eyes. "About the month's reprieve we took regarding our engagement."

This was the moment Ethen most wanted to avoid.

Seeing him turn noticeably rigid, Mary frowned for a moment, but then she gathered herself and said, "We may be engaged, but we don't know each other very well. And to be honest, you didn't really like me that much for most of our engagement."

Was that the problem after all? Ethen clenched his fists, reflecting on the past. It was true that he hadn't been in love with her a few months ago—actually, he'd been quite annoyed by her. It was to be expected that she wasn't convinced about his feelings, considering how he'd acted toward her in the past.

"That's why—"

"I'll change."

He'd been planning to let her speak and not refute anything she said, because she was right.

"Would it not be enough?"

But his lips moved on their own. He'd never loved or wanted anyone so dearly in his life. He himself hadn't known he would act this way when faced with the prospect of losing her forever.

"I'm... sorry?"

"I know that I'm not good enough to be your spouse, Lady Mary." Ethen feared what she might say in response. He could imagine her words, and that scared him. "I'm also aware that I didn't seem interested in you during our engagement."

He wanted to prevent her from saying anything at all. Seeing as he couldn't clamp his hand over her mouth or leave, he chose to speak at the risk of coming off as rude.

"When I had the opportunity, I didn't even bother to get to know you better. And I realize it must be hard to understand why I'm acting this way now. However..." Ethen hung his head. "I don't really know why I'm acting this way right now, but I want to stay engaged to you so badly that I find myself speaking illogically."

"Can you let me finish first?" Mary said, sounding taken aback. Though he couldn't see her expression because his head was down, her pale face was probably filled with confusion.

He felt dizzy at the thought of having to look at her right now. His judgment was clouded at the moment, and in the end, he made a terrible mistake.

"Is it because of Lord Vante Luce?"

"What did you say?" Mary said, sounding confused. "Why would you say something so absurd?"

"It's not that I was watching you... or anything," he said, unable to look up.

It wasn't only Ethen who was unsettled by his words.

"That was just a coincidence."

So, she did meet him. A sardonic smile appeared on his lips as he realized he'd forced her to admit the truth. "I see."

"Wait..." Mary said, flustered. "I don't know what you're thinking—actually, I do—but it's not what you think."

Ethen couldn't hear her properly. His judgment was clouded by fatigue and anxiety. "If that's the type of man you prefer... I'll do my best to be like him."

His words rendered Mary silent. He still had his head down and was unable to see her reaction.

"I don't understand what you're saying," she said after a pause.

Ethen knew that this was absurd; he and Vante were different people. He couldn't just "change" and hope to satisfy her. His head ached from lack of sleep, and the stress and fear that had plagued him for a month were controlling his brain.

"I know what you're here to talk about," he said.

"What *am* I here to talk about?" Mary said calmly.

Ethen knew the answer to this question, but he didn't want to say it out loud. "There's still about a week left," he said, not answering her. He knew it was inevitable, but now that the moment had come, he wanted to delay it as much as possible. "I'm sorry. I seem to be doing poorly today. I don't think I can converse properly in this state. How about I visit you at the mansion next time?"

"No. I want to talk today."

Despite his efforts, Mary seemed intent on talking. The moment he heard her unyielding tone, he felt like he would choke.

"Is this really the end?" he asked, his voice trembling. It was over. Tears he hadn't shed since he was a child suddenly began dropping from his eyes.

"Lord Ethen," Mary said, disconcerted to hear the tremor in his voice.

He slowly lifted his head. "Yes."

A teardrop slid from his eye the moment he looked at Mary. A mysterious look appeared on her face as she took notice of this.

"There's something I need to do today." After fixing her eyes on his face for a while, she slowly got up and approached him.

"Let me ask you a question," she said, looking down at him. "Do you like me?"

The question was hard to fathom. Surely she knew the answer. *Why is she asking me again, just as everything is about to end?*

It was a strange question, but he nodded anyway. "Yes."

"Then you don't care what I do to you?" she said, yet another mysterious question.

Ethen chose not to ask any questions of his own.

"No." He shook his head.

After hearing his answer, she slowly brought her hands to his face. He wondered what she was doing.

A moment later, he began to guess.

But why... Why is she doing this?

Unable to understand, he blinked. Mary's face slowly approached his lips as he looked up, and their silhouettes joined in the secluded garden as a cool fall breeze blew past.

The moment seemed endless and brief at the same time. Then Mary moved away and smiled at him.

"Let's go see Aria's performance together next month."

It was the brightest smile Ethen had ever seen on Mary's face.

CHAPTER ONE HUNDRED AND FORTY-TWO

I was a little nervous as I got out of the carriage. Unlike on the day of the party, the entrance to the garden looked the same as usual.

And it wasn't just the garden scenery that was waiting for me.

"Good afternoon, Lady Mary," Ethen said, walking over to me, his face calm.

I nodded. "Yes, good afternoon."

The weather was great. It was the perfect day for me to carry out what I had in mind.

"I prepared a seat in the garden since you seemed to like it last time."

"Oh, that wasn't necessary," I said, slightly surprised. I noticed then that although it was fall, roses were visible everywhere. My visit had been sudden, but he'd gone to such lengths to welcome me.

"May I escort you?" Ethen held out his hand. I wondered if it was a trick of the light that made it look like his hand was trembling. I stared down at it for a moment, then placed my hand on top of his.

"Thank you," I said, following him. The garden didn't look as fancy as it had during my last visit, but I could tell efforts had been made to make it look pretty. "It's beautiful."

"I'm relieved," Ethen said with a smile.

Soon enough, we sat down at a tea table in the middle of the garden.

"The chef said he would do his best to please you again with his food."

"I see. These look amazing."

Ethen seemed to be trying to lessen the awkward mood. "It's starting to get cold. If I'd known, I would have arranged for tea inside. Maybe you'd like to go inside—"

"It's all right. It's only fall; I can stand this kind of weather."

I was too tense to spend my time on casual small talk. *Will I be able to say the things I've come here to say? How much of it will I be able to say?*

"Is that so? Good to hear," Ethen said, looking troubled.

I guess it's about time. Doing my best not to forget the things I'd been thinking of all night, I said, "That day..."

"Yes."

"I felt uncomfortable about leaving so suddenly without saying a proper goodbye."

This needed to come before anything else. I'd been ignoring all his letters and making him worry, so I wanted to start with an apology about this.

"Don't mention it. My mother wasn't concerned at all. In fact—"

"She spoke to the House of Mirvaseba as well."

"Yes. I was told the countess promised to have a stern word with her daughter. So please don't worry about it."

"How could I not, when it has to do with me?"

Having briefly discussed that incident, I took a deep breath. "I'm here to speak to you about what we agreed on a month ago."

Ethen visibly stiffened, biting his lip. "Yes," he said.

"It hasn't been a full month yet, but I think it's best I tell you in advance." It felt uncomfortable to see him so tense, but if I didn't tell him now, things could get even worse.

"Understood," he said with a nod.

"I've been doing a lot of thinking over the past month. As you know, something unpleasant happened during that time."

"But good things happened as well," Ethen said. "I've heard that Lady Aria sang at Lady Priscilla's performance."

Undoubtedly, the entire capital had heard about her by now, so it wasn't a strange thing for him to know as well.

"You seemed happy when you saw Lady Priscilla's performance last time," he continued. "You must be proud that Lady Aria has improved to the point of performing with her."

"It's her achievement, not mine... but I was happy, yes," I said, forgetting what I'd been about to say at his compliment. It was a rather simple-minded reaction, but I was happy to have something to talk about that didn't make me feel so excruciatingly tense.

"It should be a good thing for the imperial theater that's opening soon."

"Yes. They received the best possible advertising for free," I said proudly. "They told us that she couldn't perform on stage without having something to show for herself first, so we taught them a lesson."

That performance was amazing. It would have been nice if Ethen had come, too.

"It would have been nice if you had come along..." I caught myself only after I'd blurted out something unnecessary. In truth, I'd had the opportunity to ask him to come, but I hadn't been brave enough. I bit my lip. "You would have been impressed, too, if you'd seen it."

"Yes. I'm sure I would have," Ethen said mildly. "Please tell Lady Aria I congratulated her." He was even congratulating Aria now.

"Thank you." Clearing my throat, I said, "In any case... I'd like to meet with the duchess and speak with her properly next time."

"Then I can tell my mother—"

"No. I'll contact her myself." I said, politely refusing his offer to speak with her himself. "I have something else to talk to you about." It was time I moved on to the real topic.

"About the month's reprieve we took regarding our engagement," I said after a deep breath. I'd rehearsed this line many times during the night.

"We may be engaged, but we don't know each other very well. And to be honest, you didn't really like me that much for most of our engagement." I was fidgeting with my hands under the table. "That's why—"

"I'll change," Ethen said, cutting me off before I could even get started. "Would it not be enough?"

"I'm... sorry?" I said, unable to understand. I'd reacted instinctively, but Ethen seemed to have interpreted it differently. His voice sounded very upset.

"I know that I'm not good enough to be your spouse, Lady Mary," he said quietly. "I'm also aware that I didn't seem interested in you during our engagement."

He seemed to be thinking of the way he had treated the real Mary, not me.

"When I had the opportunity, I didn't even bother to get to know you better. And I realize it must be hard to understand why I'm acting this way now. However..."

But there was no point in regretting that. I hadn't been in Mary's body then. I wondered what to do.

"I don't really know why I'm acting this way right now, but I want to stay engaged to you so badly that I find myself speaking illogically."

"Can you let me finish first?"

This isn't what I was going to talk about or what I was expecting. Can you let me talk? But his response further confused me.

"Is it because of Lord Vante Luce?"

"What did you say?" *Why are you talking about him all of a sudden?* There was no way he could have heard the rumor that had been going around at the marquess' mansion. I did my best to ignore the way my guilty heart was thumping. "Why would you say something so absurd?"

"It's not that I was watching you... or anything," he replied.

At that point, I had to accept that Ethen *had* somehow heard the rumor, though I had no idea how. Indeed, the subject of rumors often heard them last. Everyone had seemingly heard about it while I, who had been completely unaware, had been thinking about what to say. I had no idea what was happening, but setting things straight was my biggest priority.

"That was just a coincidence," I said, waving my hand in the air.

I should have a word with Hans when I get home. Why had he been blathering about me, and who had he been talking to that Ethen had heard?

"I see."

"Wait…"

Though I was flabbergasted, Ethen seemed to have already jumped to a conclusion in his head. *What do you take me for?*

I gave him a hurt look. "I don't know what you're thinking—actually, I do—but it's not what you think."

I wished he would do away with his stupid misunderstanding. Though I was serious, he didn't seem to believe me at all.

"If that's the type of man you prefer… I'll do my best to be like him."

"I don't understand what you're saying."

Please stop! I silently pleaded, sighing. Ethen was clearly more nervous than usual, but even considering that, he looked to be in poor condition today.

"I know what you're here to talk about," he said.

"What *am* I here to talk about?" I replied, a little upset because of the misunderstanding.

"There's still about a week left." He couldn't seem to hide his anxiety, his voice trembling heavily. He hadn't been able to raise his head ever since he mentioned Vante, and that made me uncomfortable.

While I'd been anxious and worried, he'd also obviously had a lot on his mind. That was why he was so unlike himself today. If I'd figured out a little more quickly what I really wanted, and if I hadn't been so obsessed with how things were "supposed to be" in this world, Ethen wouldn't have had to experience such emotions.

He seemed to think for a moment, then shook his head, still staring down. "I'm sorry. I seem to be doing poorly today. I don't think I can converse properly in this state. How about I visit you at the mansion next time?"

Now he was trying to send me away. He was right about his condition, but he was obviously using it as an excuse to send me back.

"No. I want to talk today." *Would anything change if I did as he asked and simply left? Of course not.* I'd already learned that such behavior couldn't change anything. So, I sternly refused.

CHAPTER ONE HUNDRED AND FORTY-THREE

Ethen's shoulders flinched at my firm voice, then trembled as if he were about to cry.

"Is this really the end?"

Wait, he really does look like he's about to cry. When he spoke, his voice was tearful.

Taken aback, I said, "Lord Ethen."

"Yes." He slowly raised his head. At the same time, a teardrop slid down his pale cheek.

The moment I saw it, the things I'd been planning to say to him today, which had taken me all night to think about, suddenly felt meaningless. It was not my intention to make him look this way. I never wanted or anticipated this.

What should I do right now?

"There's something I need to do today."

It didn't take me long to decide. I said something completely different from what I'd had in mind. "Let me ask you a question."

I will no longer take the roundabout way. This isn't how I wanted things to turn out.

What I wanted to find out was a very simple thing. "Do you like me?"

Ethen nodded instantly. "Yes."

"Then you don't care what I do to you?"

"No." He shook his head, again without hesitation.

This was no time to be embarrassed to show my feelings toward a man who had such complete faith and love for me. I got up and approached him.

He looked at me, wide-eyed and confused. I didn't avoid his gaze and stopped in front of him. Then, slowly, I cupped his pale face in my hands, leaned forward, and lowered my face toward his.

Maybe I'd taken too long a detour to reach this point. Certainly, it couldn't have been the ideal approach. Even what I was doing now was completely different from what I'd thought of through the night. Maybe I would regret it in a few hours.

But my life had never been that perfect in the first place.

Refusing to think any further, I pressed my lips to his.

Even if this didn't lift my curse and this kiss didn't mean anything, I was fine with that. This was the most honest thing I could do with these lips that never said what I wanted to, and the simplest way to tell him how I felt. That alone made it valuable.

The kiss was neither long nor short. I straightened up only when I felt that everything would be all right again.

I had no idea what life had in store for me now that the original plot no longer had anything to do with my life. But I was sure of one thing.

"Let's go see Aria's performance together next month."

I would no longer fear uncertainty.

That day, the cursed tongue that had made my life hell disappeared.

If Madam Lebonae was right, then the soul fragment had shattered completely. That was a lovely thing in itself, but it wasn't just my verbal freedom that I achieved that day. I'd also gained a little confidence and faith. And...

"Mary?"

Ethen's voice jerked me out of my thoughts.

"Oh." I turned around.

"What are you thinking about?"

"Just things about the past," I said, beaming at him.

It had already been over a month since that day. Ethen and I had conversed at length. Though I couldn't tell him everything about my situation, I still told him a lot. I apologized and explained that I'd never hated him. And that I'd been avoiding new feelings out of fear because I was a coward.

When I told him that I'd come to tell him I wanted to continue our engagement, his reaction astounded me.

"Lord Ethen?"

This wasn't surprising—he'd burst into tears like a child, which made his single teardrop earlier pale in comparison.

If I mentioned this to him now, he'd be embarrassed and beg me to forget. Thinking about that, I smiled at him again. "About that day you cried in front of me."

"I asked you to forget about that," he said, hanging his head and blushing. But he didn't seem to hate it.

"Does it make you cringe?"

"Huh?"

Oops. I really need to stop using modern words with him. I hurriedly corrected myself. "Is it something embarrassing? Something you'd rather forget?"

"Ah," he said with a nod. "It's embarrassing, but it's not something I want gone."

"Why not?" I already knew the answer, but I wanted to hear him say it.

"If it hadn't been for that day, I might not be here, laughing beside you."

"Hahaha! I disagree. This would have happened no matter what." My laughter, no longer as obnoxious as it had been a month ago, filled the air. "I'm sure of it." I took his hand smoothly. "Because you like me, and I like you, Ethen."

"Mary…" He blushed at the sudden confession.

After that day's prolonged conversation, we had become lovers. That was a funny thing to say considering we'd already been engaged, but it was certain that something more than a meaningless engagement bonded us now.

"Please don't be such an eyesore in public," said a familiar prickly voice as we stared lovingly into each other's eyes. "Lord Ethen, don't humor her all the time. You'll give her bad habits."

May walked through the crowd, holding a bouquet. He glared at us, though not in a hateful way.

"Why does it matter? We're engaged."

"You haven't even had a proper engagement ceremony yet. And don't you know that our parents never act like that in public, though they're married?" May said provokingly. None of what he said really bothered me, though.

"Are you sure you're not just unhappy because you don't have a partner?"

"What do you mean? Soon enough, I'll also be..." May fidgeted with the bouquet. "I'll have a lover too, one day. Just watch."

I'd been enjoying making fun of him lately. In the past, my tongue had forced me to pick fights with him, but now I was doing it of my own free will.

"You can't even talk properly in front of her."

"What are you talking about? You're completely wrong!"

Now that I had the presence of mind to look around me, I'd noticed a completely new relationship that hadn't been in the novel.

"Aria loves her work. She said she might never marry. Give it a shot if you like."

I didn't intend to try to stop him like before, but I thought Aria deserved better. He would have to live with a bit of mockery. I smiled at him mischievously.

"That's..."

"Lord May, are you and Lady Aria courting?"

Oops. I had momentarily forgotten Ethen was with me.

Belatedly pretending to be dignified again, I said, "No. He just has unrequited feelings for her."

"That's not true. S-she's a good person, but that doesn't mean I feel..." May said. But his blushing cheeks and the bouquet in his hand told a different story.

"Well... maybe you should give it a shot so you can finally give up. I'll be rooting for you," I said impishly before hiding behind Ethen.

We were in public, so May just fidgeted with his bouquet again, unable to talk back to me.

"We should have brought some flowers too," Ethen said, looking at the bouquet in May's hands.

"Don't worry. I sent multiple wreaths," I reassured him. "I sent her the prettiest bouquet in the world as well, so she'll have had her fill of flowers for the time being."

Today was the first performance at the Imperial Opera Theater, and I wanted her to look good. I'd already arranged for multiple wreaths and bouquets to be sent to her.

"The prettiest one? That one's in my room," Ethen joked, and I beamed.

He was talking about the bouquet I'd given him. I'd had Annie throw away the wreath Ethen had given me after the hunting competition, but she'd preserved it and turned it into a bouquet. When I found out, I presented it to him as a gift. The look on his face then made me want to give him surprise gifts from time to time.

"Then, it's the second prettiest," I said with a smile.

According to the novel, Mary should have been sent away to the countryside after her troublemaking, and Aria and Edville would have been preparing for an engagement.

Our futures had changed dramatically, but that didn't mean there was something wrong with our story.

"She must be nervous, right?" Ethen said.

"I don't think so. She was so chatty and excited yesterday. I had to tell her to save her voice for today and go to sleep early."

Though this world was now nothing like the one in the novel, we each had happy lives. And that was how it would be for the rest of our days.

"She'll probably sing the most beautiful song in the world today."

"I'm looking forward to it," Ethen said, laughing.

"We're so lucky to be watching from the best seats."

"That is probably thanks to my fiancée, since you have such powerful connections. Hmm, I suppose that could be described as lucky as well."

We continued to chat after we'd taken our seats. This conversation would likely go on until the lights went out and the performance began. This had become a natural part of our lives now.

"When I first met Lady Aria, I never thought such a day would come. But now we're sitting in the best seats, watching her perform," he said.

I hadn't known, either. I'd believed that the roles of the villainess, female lead, male lead, and the other potential male leads had all been set in stone.

"That's what makes life interesting."

But now, the villainess is the heroine's biggest fan, and the other potential male lead was passionately in love with her.

The female lead, who should have become the Crown Prince's wife, had become a performer in the Imperial Opera Theater, and the other characters were also living lives of their own.

"They must be about to get started."

The lights dimmed, and people moved busily about on the dark stage. The show really was about to begin.

Aria was about to become the star of the stage and the happiest singer in the entire world. She was no longer the female lead of *Beneath a Beautiful Melody* but the main singer of the Imperial Opera Theater, and there she would find her own happiness.

From my seat in the audience, I sent a round of applause toward the stage.

The End.

www.ingramcontent.com/pod-product-compliance
Lightning Source LLC
Chambersburg PA
CBHW021021310726
48969CB00006B/1491